Improbable Connections

A Mayflower Story

2

Improbable Connections

A Mayflower Story

A Historical Novel
By

Ron W Germaine

Germaine Publishing

Improbable Connections: A Mayflower Story
Copyright © 2020 by Ron W Germaine
ISBN 978-1-7343718-2-6

An eBook title is also available ISBN 978-1-7343718-3-3

Cover design: Acrylic painting by Heather Germaine

DEDICATION

This book is dedicated to my five beautiful grandchildren, Hannah, Sophia, Caleb, Isla, and Amelia Germaine. May the faith, hope, love, and resilience our Mayflower relatives lived out be real throughout your lives.

Table of Contents

8

ACKNOWLEDGMENTS

My mother, Nellie (Dowse-Sims) Germaine, planted the seed for this book when she talked to me about 'our relatives who came over on the Mayflower.' While support has not been found for direct ancestry, evidence shows a 'cousin' relationship to Mayflower passengers Mary (Chilton) Winslow and Elisabeth (Tilley) Howland. I will always treasure Nellie's love of learning and her encouragement to me to stretch beyond my comfort zone.

I am grateful to Caleb Johnson and the research posted on his website, *MayflowerHistory.com*. There, I learned much about Mayflower passengers and their relationships with one another. Nathaniel Philbrick's book, *Mayflower: A story of courage, community, and war*, was also a valuable source of historical documentation.

I am grateful to those who read initial manuscripts of this book and offered valuable counsel. IndieReader provided a useful critique of an early version of the manuscript. Other readers providing helpful feedback included Christal Peters, Scott Bergstrome, Lesley Kay, Elaine Senack, CJ Maloney, Karen Ryan, and Heather Germaine. Thank you, Heather, for brainstorming with me about characters, the title, chapter sequence, painting the picture for the cover, and for encouraging me to continue writing in the face of major distractions.

Prologue

James Charles Stuart was crowned King James VI of Scotland in July of 1567. With the death of childless Elizabeth I in 1603, James, the closest heir to Elizabeth, became King James I of England, Scotland, and Ireland. Monarchs from biblical times saw themselves as having a divine right to govern, and James was no exception. He wrote a book to outline the theological argument for his belief, *The true law of free monarchies*. As King of England, Scotland, and Ireland, James was not only the head of state but also the head of the Church of England, which had split with the Catholic Church some 50 years earlier. Not recognizing any separation of church and state, King James believed that active opposition to the Church of England was subversive to his authority.

A sizeable group within the Church of England opposed some of the traditions practiced by the Church and clergy. Called Puritans, this group thought the Church should have fewer Catholic traditions, which included use of the Book of Common Prayer, ceremonial dress of clergy, use of the sign of the cross, and kneeling to receive Communion. Puritans also thought the hierarchical structure and authority of the Church of England was too much like that of the Catholic Church. They believed that in matters of worship, even the King as head of the Church of England should not dictate how individuals must worship, nor should the King or other church leaders prescribe what individual church members must believe. Many Puritans remained members of the Church of England to try to influence the Church from within. They saw their beliefs as superior to the beliefs and practices of others within the Church who saw no need for change. Humility was not their strongest virtue.

A smaller number of Puritans did not think the King would ever allow the Church of England to change sufficiently for them to worship in the purely biblical way they deemed appropriate. This group of Puritans withdrew from the Anglican Church and formed their own congregations, often meeting in one another's homes. They were known as Separatists. While Separatists were very committed to their beliefs, they attempted to live out what they believed in a spirit of humility.

The King and most priests within the Church of England demanded conformity to their authority and forms of worship. King James not only felt insulted when Separatists withdrew from the Church to form their own congregations but saw their actions as treasonous. He made a lack of attendance at parish churches a crime punishable by jail or even death. Additionally, leaving England because of disagreements with the Church was also seen as traitorous. In England in the 1600s, there was no such thing as separation of church and state.

Groups of Separatists were hounded by authorities who sometimes watched their houses for illegal church meetings. Some Separatists were jailed and their property confiscated. Such persecution turned the thoughts of Separatist leaders toward finding another country where they could worship freely. A prominent Separatist, William Brewster, had been to Holland and knew firsthand of the open-mindedness there towards various systems of belief. It was, in fact, the only country in Europe that tolerated diverse religious beliefs. Since Holland was relatively close to England, and the industry and relative prosperity of the country made the likelihood of finding employment higher than anywhere else, it became the first refuge for Separatists outside of England. John and Joan Tilley and daughter Elisabeth were part of a group of Separatists who emigrated to Holland – and later to America - seeking religious freedom.

Following the arrival of the Separatists in America, tolerance – if not wholly charitable relationships - characterized much of the initial contact between the English and Native Americans. However, it did not last. Details of that story are heartbreaking, and should not be forgotten – but they are for another time, not included in the narrative that follows.

Real Historical Characters

Mayflower passengers: All Mayflower passengers and crew mentioned are real historical characters. The most general information about them in this book is based on factual evidence. For example, there is documentation that the Tilley family was from Henlow in the county of Bedfordshire, England; they lived in Leiden; they sailed on the Mayflower to Plymouth; and Elisabeth's parents died not long after arriving at Plymouth. Specific information about their day-to-day lives is fictional.

Elisabeth Tilley: Elisabeth is the daughter of John and Joan Tilley. Documentation shows she was born in 1607 in Henlow, Bedfordshire, England. We know she was the only survivor of her family after the first winter in Plymouth. She married John Howland in 1623 before her 16th birthday. I have spelled her name with an "s" rather than a "z" in honor of my granddaughter, Sophia Elisabeth, who was born in England.

John Tilley: John was Elisabeth's father. He died during the first winter in Plymouth.

Joan Tilley: Joan was Elisabeth's mother. She died during the first winter in Plymouth

Samoset: Samoset is a Native American, the father of fictional Hurit, and husband of fictional Wawestseka. Samoset's name means, 'he who walks over much.' Some English writers referred to him as 'Somerset,' perhaps because they knew of a county in England by that name. He was a sagamore or sachem, a 'lesser chief' who served as an advisor to the great chief of the Wampanoag tribe, Massasoit. Samoset was from Pemaquid Point in what is now Maine, and a member of the Abenaki tribe. He was the first Native American to meet the Pilgrims, saying the famous, "Welcome Englishmen." He introduced them a few days later to Squanto and Massasoit.

Squanto (or Tisquantum): Squanto was a Native American from Patuxet, the site on which the Pilgrims built Plymouth. Squanto was kidnapped several years before the Pilgrims' arrival, sold as a slave in Spain, somehow made his way to England, and eventually came back to his home in Patuxet. His village was wiped out by disease about two years before he returned. While in England, Squanto became fluent in English, and on his return, served as an interpreter/negotiator between Native Americans and the English settlers. He died in November 1622.

John Smith: Captain Smith was an English sailing captain who sailed on an expedition in 1614 to the area north of the Hudson River, and named it New England. A second ship captained by Thomas Hunt accompanied him. Before his voyage with Thomas Hunt, Smith governed the English colony at Roanoke, Virginia.

Thomas Hunt: Captain Hunt was an English sailing captain who kidnapped Squanto and about 26 other Native Americans and sold them as slaves in Spain.

John Slany: John Slany was a businessman, financier, and shipbuilder who lived in the Cornhill area of London, England. He invested in the East India Company and was treasurer of the Company of Adventurers and Planters of London and Bristol. The company hoped to earn a profit from fishing, furs, and settlements in North America.

Sir Walter Raleigh: Raleigh was an English adventurer who served under Elisabeth I and James I. He was eventually put to death by King James for treason.

Reverend Ashbold: William Ashbold was Rector of St. Michaels Church, Cornhill from 1587-1622, the time during which Squanto would have been in England. The church was part of the Church of England.

King James: James VI of Scotland, born June 19, 1566. In 1603 he followed Elisabeth I to the throne, becoming King James I of England, Scotland, and Ireland. He wrote treatises on the divine right of kings, witchcraft, biblical themes, and set into motion a translation of the Bible known as the King James Version.

John Mason: John Mason was the Governor of the settlement at Cuper's Cove, Newfoundland, at the time Squanto was sent from England to help expand settlement and the fur trade.

Thomas Dermer: Captain Dermer was an English sailing captain stationed at Cuper's Cove in Newfoundland. He sailed from Cuper's Cove to New England with Squanto aboard his ship.

Massasoit: Massasoit was from the Pokanoket tribe of Native Americans. He provided leadership to a group of 8-10 bands in the New England area. Together they were called the Wampanoag Nation and included the Patuxet tribe to which Squanto belonged.

Rembrandt van Rijn: Rembrandt was a Dutch artist, born in Leiden, Holland in 1606. While a real person, Rembrandt's friendship with Elisabeth is fictional. His parents, Harmen and Neeltgen van Rijn and his sister, Lysbeth, were real people.

John Robinson: John Robinson was the pastor of the Leiden congregation of Separatists.

Master Reynolds: Master Reynolds was captain of the Speedwell, the ship that was intended to accompany the Mayflower to Virginia, but was found to be unseaworthy.

Missy and Sadie: Two dogs, a springer spaniel and a mastiff, brought from Leiden, Holland to Plymouth by John Goodman. The dogs' names are fictional, but the dogs came to Plymouth on the Mayflower.

Master Christopher Jones: Master Jones was the captain of the Mayflower.

John Howland: John was a Mayflower passenger indentured to John Carver, the first governor of the Plymouth colony. John was born in Fenstanton, Huntingdon, England, in the mid to late 1590s. He married Elisabeth Tilley in New England, likely in 1623.

Fictional Characters

Hurit: Hurit is the daughter of a real person, Samoset, and her fictional mother, Wawestseka. In the novel, Hurit and Elisabeth become friends. Hurit's name means 'Beautiful, attractive, or fine-looking.'

Wawestseka: Wawestseka is the mother of Hurit and Samoset's fictional wife. Her name means 'Pretty Woman.'

Juan Batista: Juan is a businessman who manufactured gunpowder in Malaga, Spain. He purchased Squanto as a slave from Captain Thomas Hunt.

George Smyth: George is a solicitor in London. Before moving to London, George lived in Henlow and was a friend of John Tilley's. He did legal work for John.

Ahanu: Ahanu is a member of the Pokanoket tribe who lived in Sowams. He was a 'runner' who carried communication to other bands in the Wampanoag nation. He married Hurit. His name means 'he who laughs.'

Definitions

Narragansetts: The Narragansetts were a Native American tribe who were rivals to Massasoit and his Wampanoag confederacy. They lived to the southwest of the Pokanokets along Narragansett Bay.

Nausets: The Nausets were a Native American band that lived on Cape Cod. They were the people from whom a Mayflower exploratory party stole corn in November 1620.

Patuxets: The Patuxets were a band of Native Americans who lived at the site of the Pilgrims' colony at Plymouth. They were wiped out by disease about two years before the Pilgrims' arrival. Squanto was the last surviving member of the Patuxet band of Native Americans.

Saints: Saints is the term the Separatists used to refer to themselves on the Mayflower. It distinguished them from other passengers on the voyage who did not share the same religious beliefs. Those other passengers were referred to as Strangers.

Sagamore, Sachem: Both terms refer to 'lesser chiefs' from Native American bands that made up the Wampanoag nation in the New England area. Sagamores or Sachems advised the great Wampanoag chief, Massasoit, and recognized his leadership. Samoset was one of Massasoit's sagamores or sachems.

Separatists: Separatists were Puritans who chose to leave the Church of England (the Anglican Church) because they thought the Church had many traditions that did not follow scripture as carefully as they thought necessary. They thought the Church of England was too much like the Catholic Church.

Sowams: Sowams was the village where Massasoit lived, about a two-day walk southwest of Plymouth.

Strangers: Strangers were passengers who traveled on the Mayflower, but were not Separatist-Puritans. They were passengers chosen by English investors because they were able to pay for their passage, and therefore help fund the voyage.

Wampanoags: The Wampanoags were a confederation of Native American tribes that extended from Massachusetts to as far north as Rhode Island. Massasoit was the grand chief of the Wampanoags from about 1615 through 1660. Wampanoag has the meaning 'Easterners.'

PART I: BIRTH OF ELISABETH AND HURIT

Chapter 1. 1607: An Ocean Apart

The cry of a new-born baby echoed within the home of Joan and John Tilley. John gently wiped the face of his new daughter and lifted her to his wife's breast as she lay on a straw mattress. "We have a daughter, Joan," he told her. He wrapped the new baby with a light wool blanket.

"Let's call her Elisabeth," Joan said with a weak smile. It was a warm summer evening in Henlow, in the county of Bedfordshire, England. John knelt by the bed, keeping Joan cool with a leather fan and periodically placing a damp cloth on her forehead.

Their home was a small, three-room stone structure, with a glass window in each room. A fireplace was the sole source of heat for cooking and warmth. The floor consisted of flat stones held together by mortar. In the room that served as the family bedroom, a thatched carpet of woven reeds covered part of the stone floor. Tallow candles provided light at nighttime.

As Joan held her newborn, and John sat beside her, their eyes met, and both knew the feelings of hope and fear that were unexpressed. The fear was that their new little one might not survive her first year. Four of their previous newborns had died before their first birthday. John expressed their hope in a prayer, "May Elisabeth not only survive, but may she also be strong, and thrive."

~

On the same July evening, three thousand, three hundred miles to the west in what is now known as Pemaquid Point in southeast Maine, Wawestseka and her husband Samoset heard a similar cry as they welcomed their own new baby.

Samoset carefully wrapped the infant in a soft beaver skin and placed the baby at her mother's breast. "She looks like you, Wawestseka. She's beautiful," Wawestseka held her daughter, who quickly began nursing. After a few moments, she looked up at Samoset, and with a tired but warm smile said, "Yes, she is beautiful, and we will help her to be wise. Let's call her Hurit."

Their home was dome-shaped, 14 feet in circumference, and eight feet at the highest point. It was made from saplings tied together with walnut bark and covered with cattail mats. An opening in the middle of the roof at the highest point allowed smoke to escape from the central cooking and heating fire.

Hurit and her family were members of the Abenaki tribe, one of many Native American groups that made up the Algonquin nation. Perhaps because they were one of the easternmost tribes, their name had the meaning, 'people of the dawn.'

~

On the day Samoset's daughter was born, his traveling partner and friend Squanto, from Patuxet, was with him. The two were soon to embark on an annual discovery trip. Each year they traveled together between present-day Maine in the north to as far as Rhode Island in the south, visiting other tribes to learn about trade opportunities, crops, movement of game, and convey messages between tribal leaders. They shared the findings from their travels at a leadership council.

Samoset proudly showed Squanto his new daughter. "Look how perfect she is!" Samoset exclaimed. Squanto held the infant briefly. As he looked at her small form, he said, "Little Hurit, may you not only be beautiful but may you find strong friendships and be a good communicator like your father."

The date was July 15th, 1607. Neither set of parents nor Squanto could possibly imagine the improbable connections that over the next 14 years would bring the girls together.

PART II: SQUANTO'S STORY

Chapter 2. 1614: Captain Hunt

Captain Thomas Hunt was in a foul mood.

He had sailed from England to the Hudson River area of North America on a voyage with Captain John Smith. Their expedition was financed by businessmen from the Company of Adventurers and Planters of London and Bristol. The investors commissioned the two captains to trade for furs which were in high demand in England, look for sites suitable for establishing a colony that could become a headquarters for trade, and bring back information about new sources of gold and copper.

Even though Hunt commanded his own ship, Captain Smith carried final authority over the expedition. Smith named the area they explored north of the Hudson River, New England. Both captains traded with Native Americans for furs while the fish they netted dried onshore. They found no evidence of gold or copper mines, but furs were plentiful, and Native Americans were eager to trade furs for cloth and metal goods. Smith loaded the holds on his own ship with furs. He was now anxious to deliver his high-value cargo to English investors. Demand for furs – particularly beaver pelts – was high in England and Europe. Beavers had once thrived in Europe but were now almost extinct. "Our investors are anxious for our enterprise to show a profit," he told Hunt. "The fish drying will take a few weeks yet. I will take the furs to England. When the fish have finished drying, load your holds. You'll get the best price for dried fish in Malaga. We'll share our combined proceeds when you get back to London."

Captain Hunt nodded assent, but he didn't like the plan. "That scoundrel!" he thought. "Smith will take the cargo with the highest return and leave me to load and handle smelly fish!" Hunt knew that Smith and his crew would be paid handsomely for furs. He brooded about the difference in value between Smith's cargo of furs and the cargo of dried fish he would now have to load. Even though profits from the two ships were to be shared, Hunt feared his portion would be less than Smith's. The more he thought about the potential difference, the angrier he became.

That evening Captain Hunt sat in his cabin, his anger simmering. As it did, an idea began to form in his mind. He could enhance the cargo value quite easily. He would bribe savages – Native Americans – to load his ship, and when they were finished, he would carry out a plan he knew other captains had employed. He had heard of the demand for fish in Malaga, Spain, and he knew of another cargo that could bring a handsome profit there!

Chapter 3. 1614: Samoset and Squanto

Hurit was in her seventh spring. She loved to sit close to her father, Samoset, especially when he talked with the men of their village. Being with her father made Hurit feel special. Very few men allowed children to be with them when they gathered to share stories. "Stay close to me and just listen when we are with the men," he had told her.

Hurit was especially enjoying today. Her father had returned home from a scouting mission, and he allowed her to accompany him throughout the day and evening. He had brought a friend, Squanto, who was from the Patuxet band to the south. The two men often traveled together to learn about movements of game, find out how crops were doing in other areas, and communicate with other tribes about trading opportunities.

This afternoon's conversation among the men was especially interesting. Hurit listened quietly as her father and Squanto described their experiences. While the stories the men shared were always fascinating and sometimes funny, she noticed today that their voices were more hushed, and the men leaned in.

"We met the captains of two floating islands," Samoset said.

"They are still south of here near Patuxet," he reported. Their men are fishing, and some are trading for furs. Both captains are English," Squanto noted.

Both English and French ships came great distances across the ocean to harvest fish from their region and trade for furs. Some had even tried to build settlements. These travelers came in ships so large the men often referred to them as floating islands. The sailors had loud weapons that were loud, shooting flame and smoke.

Samoset's and Squanto's interactions on their latest trip had been with the Englishmen. "They are short, have white skin and hair on their faces," Samoset stated. "They have two kinds of weapons - long metal swords and, of course, guns. I saw one of the sailors shoot a deer from a distance of a hundred paces. We could never do that with our bows and arrows!"

"The English have a drink they call beer," Squanto added. "They shared it with some of our people when they were trading. The beer has a taste we didn't like at first," he continued. "However, two men from my village appeared to like it a lot. After drinking a few mugs, their speech was slurred; their balance didn't seem so good."

During their travels together, Samoset and Squanto met and talked with captains from several sailing vessels. They not only knew the captains' names but had learned some of their language – enough that Samoset and Squanto used it in conversation with one another. In describing their conversations with sailors, the two acted out how they sometimes communicated. The Abenaki men hooted as Samoset and Squanto physically demonstrated the meaning of some of the English words. "They ask us many questions about our land, and about rivers or inlets that could take their boats further inland or even to a western sea," said Samoset. "And they almost always speak of their great king who lives on the other side of the ocean."

Though the English words her father mentioned sounded peculiar to Hurit, she listened carefully. She tried to imagine what the children of the sailors might be like. What if she met them? Could she talk with them like her father talked to men from the floating islands? What would the children look like? Could she play with them? What if those children should come to the forests where she lived?

As the men's conversations ebbed and flowed, Squanto finally said he must get some rest. "I must leave early in the morning for my village," he said. "The English Captain, Hunt, asked me to choose my strongest friends to load dried fish on his ship. He agreed to pay us with metal axes and knives," said Squanto. "The men who will work with me are anxious to get those tools."

Had Squanto known Captain Hunt's plan, he and the other Patuxet men would have been less eager to help him load. They would have used their own means of ending his deceptive, malevolent plot.

Chapter 4. 1614: Kidnapped

At dawn five days later, Squanto was back at Patuxet. Racks of dried fish were ready to be transported from the shore to Captain Hunt's boat. Squanto, with nineteen other Patuxet men and seven Nauset friends from nearby Cape Cod helped the English sailors pack the dried fish into dories. They rowed out to Captain Hunt's ship, used nets and ropes to raise the fish onto the deck, and then packed it below decks in the hold. The work was hard, but Captain Hunt had laid fine-looking axes and knives on the deck for Squanto and the others to see. "Soon, these will be yours," he told the men. At the end of each day, he provided the workers with a tall mug of beer. Near the end of the fourth day, they started packing the last load of dried fish in the hold of Captain Hunt's ship.

While Squanto and his men were still stacking the fish below deck, they noticed a slightly different motion of the ship. Concerned, Squanto started up the ladder to see what was happening, but before he reached the deck a sailor pointed a gun. Another sailor kicked hard at the ladder, and Squanto fell back in the hold. Two other sailors quickly pulled the ladder from the hold, while still others slammed the hatch shut. "No!" Squanto shouted. The hold was dark, and fear gripped the men. Squanto and the 26 men with him immediately knew they were prisoners.

A cruel smile formed on Captain Hunt's face. "Congratulations, men! We did it!" he said to his crew. "Our cargo just doubled in value. Until we reach Malaga, Spain, each of you will receive an extra daily shot of brandy."

The sailors cheered. With sails already hoisted, the ship with its cargo and captives was underway.

Chapter 5. 1614-1615: Squanto goes to Spain

The ship's hold was not only dark. It already reeked of fish and soon of human waste. Some of the men were sick. Their rations of water and food were infrequent. Hunger and thirst were constant companions. Thoughts of families and friends back in Patuxet brought sadness. Their relatives would know the men had been taken. Surely, they would bring revenge on other Englishmen who dared come ashore.

Squanto's spirit of optimism kept him from succumbing to discouragement. Despite the squalid conditions, he was grateful to be alive. He wondered what lay ahead. He had heard from the English captains about their land across the ocean. He imagined meeting the king of whom they spoke, seeing houses and castles made of stone, and other mysteries they talked of. He related stories to his companions told him by Englishmen, doing his best to encourage them and raise their spirits. They were understandably fearful of what lay ahead. The awful voyage was to last almost seven weeks.

In the fall of 1614, Captain Hunt's ship arrived in Malaga, Spain. For several days, Squanto and his companions sensed they might be near the end of their voyage. The ocean swell had lessened. The shouts of sailors had increased as had the scurrying of boots on the deck. Finally, they felt the jar of the boat as it bumped against a dock.

It took another day before the Native Americans were brought out of the hold. The sunlight was so bright they needed to shade their eyes, but the warmth of the sun felt wonderful. Captain Hunt's sailors brought water on deck so the captives could wash away the stench of their voyage. The sailors also brought food on board for them to eat. It was a fruit the Native Americans had never seen, and after observing the sailors peeling the fruit before eating it, they did the same and enjoyed the sweet, clean taste of oranges. Squanto did not recognize the shouts of men onshore. "Most of the sounds we hear are not English or French," he told his friends. "I have no idea where we are."

That night Squanto and his friends slept on the deck. The first thought each man had was of how to escape. But hope for escape was fleeting. Where would they go if they fled? As if to wipe out additional thoughts of flight, four sailors armed with rifles guarded them: one on each side of the ship, one near the bow, and the other near the stern.

Morning came and with it, another rude surprise. All twenty-seven Native American prisoners were tied with rope that joined them in a long line. Sailors roughly knotted the rope around each man so that all had to walk at the same pace in the same direction. They were led down a plank onto the dock, along the Paseo del Muello Uno and Calle Molina Lario, and in sight of a growing crowd, up the steps of a rough platform in front of the Alcazaba fortress.

Spectators gathered to gawk at the 'savages' and to watch the auction that was about to begin. They were impressed at how tall and well-proportioned this new set of slaves were. They noticed the straight, black, shoulder-length hair, some having it tied or knotted behind their necks. None had facial hair, and they wore only a cloth about their waist. One by one, the Native Americans were sold to various bidders. Squanto was claimed about halfway through the bidding process. The man who bought him exchanged payment with Captain Hunt and hurried Squanto away from his companions. It was the last time he saw his friends or Captain Hunt.

Chapter 6. 1615: A Chance Meeting in Spain

Juan Batista felt satisfied. For several months he had been looking for reliable help for the tedious work of making gunpowder. Paying local laborers ate into his profits, and the quality of powder produced was often not as good as it should have been. He was hopeful the slave he just purchased would be his answer.

"It is important to pound the ingredients to a fine powder," Batista explained to Squanto. Recognizing Squanto would not understand his verbal communication, Batista showed him an example of what the finished product must be like. Squanto nodded in understanding.

Good gunpowder required fine, evenly-ground ingredients. When that was the case, the gunpowder burned quickly and provided greater firepower. Batista prided himself in producing and selling high-quality gunpowder. However, recently, a buyer had complained that the quality of his product had declined. Batista was determined to correct that problem. "If this new slave works out," he thought, "he will be the solution to my problems of quality." And to no one in particular, he continued out loud, "And I like the price of his labor: just food."

Squanto's task was to use a heavy, hardwood pestle to grind the gunpowder ingredients: saltpeter, charcoal, and sulfur. Batista demonstrated the process and watched Squanto as he began the pounding. Batista checked frequently during the first few days to make sure the powder produced was sufficiently fine. Squanto found the work repetitive and uninspiring but developed a routine to make the job tolerable. His thoughts frequently went to his home and family. He imagined meeting them again. And he thought of the stories he would relate to Samoset and others about his capture as they sat around an evening fire.

Batista was pleased with the quality of gunpowder ingredients Squanto produced. A bonus was that Squanto was low maintenance and had a pleasant disposition. Shortly after sunrise and before sunset each day, Batista brought Squanto to the front deck of his house for a meal. In the evening after supper, the two often sat on the same deck enjoying a cup of wine. Having communicated with English and French ship captains, Squanto was familiar with signing communication, and how to build a basic vocabulary in another language. He began to pick up Spanish words from Batista. Squanto learned that Batista also spoke rudimentary English. Batista was amazed to discover that the slave who had come from the New World understood more English than he did. Slowly and at times, painstakingly, Squanto shared the story of how he and his friend Samoset met English fishing boat captains and over time, learned elements of their language. He told Batista about his home and family across the ocean.

In the spring of 1615, six months after Squanto came to Malaga, a guest came to stay with Batista. It was evening when the man arrived, and Batista and Squanto were sitting on the porch sipping wine. "Welcome, Master Slany!" Batista said in English. "Es bueno verlo de nuevo, Señor Batista," the man responded in Spanish. "It is good to see you again, my friend," he repeated in English.

"Come, sit with us here," said Batista. "Join us in a cup of wine."

While Batista went inside to get a cup for Slany, Slany turned to what he recognized as Batista's slave, wondering what to say. Squanto looked at Slany, smiled, and said in unmistakable English, "Welcome, Englishman." The visitor could hardly believe his ears. The visitor was even more incredulous as Batista returned and told Slany he had bought Squanto locally from a sailing captain who had come from the New World.

Squanto was at work the next morning when Batista escorted Slany on a tour of his gunpowder manufacturing process. They did not spend much time with Squanto, but Squanto clearly understood Slany to say, "I want to talk with you this evening."

Slany had come to Spain at Batista's request. Batista's supply of saltpeter for manufacturing gunpowder was, at best, sporadic. Ever since the defeat of the Spanish Armada in 1588 and later hostilities with the Dutch, Spain was no longer the main power on the oceans. "You and the Dutch now dominate the oceans where our Spanish ships once ruled," said Batista. "It was easy for me to buy saltpeter at one time, but now the supplies from Spanish providers are drying up. I hope we can find a way to negotiate a steady supply of saltpeter for the right price," said Batista. An additional thought in his mind was, "If I can do that, my business will flourish."

"I may be able to help with that," said Slany. One of Slany's business interests was the British East India Company. On this current trip, he was representing the company to find additional markets for the primary commodities they brought from India: saltpeter, silk, dyes, tea, and spices.

But meeting Squanto meant much more to Slany than Batista would ever know. In a separate business venture before coming to Spain, Slany, along with Sir Frances Bacon and Sir Percival Willoughby, had formed The Company of Adventurers and Planters of London. The purpose of their new company was to earn profits from colonizing projects in Newfoundland and other parts of the New World. "This Native American would add immeasurable value to our Newfoundland enterprise," he thought to himself. "He could communicate with English captains and settlers…he knows the land, and how to survive…he could be our ticket to higher profits in a shorter time."

"I think there's something we both need here, Juan," Slany continued. "You need a guaranteed supply of saltpeter," he said. "I can provide that for you. My company has committed ships to sail regularly to India, and we have suppliers there who can easily meet your needs for saltpeter. But to guarantee that supply for you, you must give me something I need."

Batista looked at Slany. "What do I have that is so enticing to you?" he asked.

"Your man, Squanto," responded, Slany.

"Why do you need him?" asked Batista. "I don't want to lose him. He's working out very well for me here."

"Our king very much wants to meet people from the New World," Slany said. "He is interested in establishing settlements there, and Squanto could prove useful in making that happen." Slany avoided mentioning his real reason for wanting to take Squanto with him. He believed Squanto would be a shorter route to profits for his Company of Adventurers and Planters in the New World.

Though at first reluctant to lose Squanto, Batista was persuaded by Slany's arguments. "With a steady supply of lower-cost raw materials, your gunpowder business will grow enough for you to buy many slaves to replace Squanto. You will get a guaranteed supply of saltpeter at half the price you currently pay," Slany pointed out. "I will earn a profit from the trade with India, and perhaps King James will look favorably on me for introducing to him a native from the New World. We both get something we need." While that was true, Slany was primarily interested in how Squanto could support his company.

The two men came to an agreement, and the following morning drew up a contract that both men signed. They walked to Squanto's work area, where Slany gave Squanto a warm smile and handshake. Squanto clearly understood Slany's statement, "You will come with me to England to meet King James." He was surprised, delighted, and relieved. Now he would go with this man to the land of which the fishing boat captains spoke and meet their leader. Intuitively, Squanto sensed that this opportunity was a step in the right direction. "Could this be the first step in returning to my home?" he thought.

"I will go with you," Squanto said to Slany, though in fact, he really had no choice. "I would like to meet your King."

Chapter 7. 1615: Squanto in England

The voyage from Malaga, Spain to London, England was on Slany's ship, Discovery. The journey was about 14 days, about a month shorter than what Squanto had experienced on the trip from New England to Spain. However, more importantly to Squanto, Slany did not treat him as a captive. Squanto had his own small cabin next to Master John Slany's cabin. Even the sailors treated Squanto respectfully. He and Slany shared meals.

During dinner one evening, Slany told Squanto, "Captain John Smith sailed this very ship to your country to begin a settlement in Jamestown, Virginia."

"I have not heard of Virginia, but I did meet a Captain John Smith," responded Squanto. "He and another Captain sailed into the bay near my home. Captain Smith was honorable in his trade with us, but the man with him, Captain Hunt, was not. He is the one who tricked my friends and me. He trapped us in his ship while we were loading his fish. He brought us to Magdala, where Batista bought me."

Slany took every possible opportunity to converse with Squanto, asking about his home area in New England, about other Native Americans who lived in the region, how they lived, what they ate, and what crops they grew. He asked about the weather and seasons, and about contacts and trading with Englishmen and Frenchmen. Slany was patient with Squanto's limited grasp of English and was careful to take time to repeat and explain words. Squanto was a willing student, and his competence in understanding and speaking the language rapidly increased. Slany was impressed at how quickly Squanto grasped English. The more they talked together, the more confident he was that Squanto would be invaluable to his Company of Adventurers in their quest to profit from trade and settlement in the New World.

Their ship, the Discovery, sailed up the Thames River on the rising tide, stopping at Blackwall, where the East India Company was constructing docks and a shipbuilding yard. "This is an excellent mooring site because it is so well protected by that jetty," Slany told Squanto, pointing at Blackwall Rock. "We will travel by horse and carriage from here to London." Stopping at Blackwall meant the ship could avoid the longer journey up the Thames around the Isle of Dogs, and up to the Tower Bridge in London.

Chapter 8. 1615: Meeting Sir Walter Raleigh

Upon disembarking, Slany and Squanto walked together toward another ship Slany recognized. It was being loaded with supplies. I know where to find the captain of that ship," said Slany. "I want you to meet him." The two walked a short distance to a tavern called the Signe of the Three Mariners. Upon entering, a voice boomed out, "Welcome back Master Slany!"

"Good to see you, Sir Walter," responded Slany. "I'm glad to see your home is no longer the Tower of London. No doubt the Three Mariners is a more pleasant place!"

"Our good King James wants gold more than he wants me in chains," replied Sir Walter Raleigh with a laugh. "He has directed me to lead another expedition to southern waters in search of the golden city, El Dorado."

"And who comes with you?" Raleigh asked, looking at Squanto.

"This is Squanto, who has come to us from New England, by way of Spain," replied Slany. He will work for our Company of Adventurers and Planters to establish commerce in Newfoundland – and perhaps beyond."

"I'm happy to meet you, Squanto," said Sir Walter, as the two shook hands. You're working with a sagacious and generous man." Squanto did not yet know the depth of meaning in the English words Sir Walter used, but understood the respect between the two men.

"I had a strong friendship with Manteo, a native who came from our

Roanoke colony to visit England some 20 years ago," Raleigh continued. "You remind me of him. He learned English, and we learned some of his language. He was a great assistance to my men and the early colonists in Virginia."

In the 1590s, Queen Elizabeth granted Sir Walter Raleigh a charter to establish a colony in North America. Though Raleigh himself never went to the new territory, his men built a settlement on Roanoke Island. "Be sure to name the new colony 'Virginia'" Sir Walter had instructed his men. Our 'Virgin Queen,' Elizabeth, will appreciate that name!" And sure enough, the Queen granted a charter to Sir Walter as a way of showing her pleasure with him. She also bestowed knighthood and other royal favors on him.

A few years later, Elizabeth learned that Sir Walter had married one of her court maids. The discovery made her furious. She imprisoned them both in the Tower of London. However, when new rumors surfaced about gold in lands of the South Atlantic, the Queen released Sir Walter. "I need you to find that source of gold," she told him. "You are more valuable to me in that search than you are wasting away in the Tower."

Sir Walter's mission was unsuccessful, and a new monarch, King James I, came to the throne. Shortly after James' coronation, Sir Walter was implicated in a plot to oust the new king. At trial, Raleigh was sentenced to death and again thrown into the Tower of London. But fresh rumors about gold in El Dorado surfaced and King James could not resist. He freed Raleigh. "You're like a cat with nine lives," he told Raleigh. "Go! But be sure you find the gold!" Raleigh was now preparing for that voyage.

Slany and Squanto joined Sir Walter Raleigh for dinner at the tavern. During the meal, Slany probed Sir Walter about his thoughts of starting a new settlement in the New World. "It will not be easy," Raleigh said. "Not long ago, I heard that the Frenchman, Champlain lost more than half of his settlers during their first winter Quebec."

At the mention of Champlain, Squanto interjected, "A French captain, Champlain came to our village when I was a young boy. His ship sailed into the bay in front of my home. My father and some other men from our village rowed out to the ship because it ran aground at low tide. The ship refloated at high tide, and the next day, the captain and some of his men came to check out the river near our town. They were disappointed because it was not large enough for their ship to enter. Soon after, they left our bay."

"It was very likely the same Captain Champlain," said Raleigh. "His Quebec settlement was a disaster during their first winter. Sixteen of the twenty-five or so people with him died. New colonists who go to any location in the New World will need to be courageous, determined, and resourceful if they are to survive beyond a few months or years."

Squanto wondered to himself why so many English and French died when they came to his homeland. He and his people knew the land. They were in harmony with their environment, knew where and how to grow corn and squash. They adapted their dwellings to the seasons. The English and French did not understand such ways, he reasoned.

Raleigh continued, "It wasn't only the French who had difficulty establishing a presence across the ocean. Many of our Virginia colonists died during their first attempts at settlement – though it had more to do with insufficient food resources than cold. The colonists who survived and stayed on in Roanoke had a very uneasy relationship with the natives. Captain John Smith governed the Roanoke settlement for a time. He and the settlers struggled to feed themselves. It seems the relationship with the natives didn't get off to a very good start. And then there was that gunpowder explosion that just about killed Smith. Poor man! He had to return to England for medical help."

At the mention of Captain Smith, Squanto could not help but ask, "Is this the same Captain John Smith, who sailed to my homeland with Captain Thomas Hunt to search for furs and fish?'

Raleigh looked incredulous, and Slany smiled and nodded. "It's the same one, alright." Then looking at Raleigh, Slany commented, "We couldn't make up this scenario. Squanto has met almost as many sailing captains as we know!" The men laughed together, then Squanto became somber.

"My people provided many furs for Captain Smith," said Squanto, "and he provided iron shovels, axes, and knives for us. He was a good man. When Captain Smith left, Captain Hunt asked for our help to load dried fish on his ship in return for additional iron axes. We trusted him because Captain Smith had dealt honestly with us. But when we loaded the last of the fish in Captain Hunt's hold, the sailors closed the hatch and held us captive. We did not come willingly to Magdala, Spain."

The three men sat in silence for a time, each man in his own way marveling at the improbable connections that led each individual to sharing a meal at the Signe of the Three Mariners.

When they finished, Raleigh invited Slany and Squanto to stay overnight in the guests' quarters at his home. "I know you want to be on your way to London, but you can arrange for a carriage for the journey this evening, and have a good rest before you leave in the morning. I recommend you stop by my tailor one street over. He will have some clothes for Squanto so that he is not such a curiosity in England."

Chapter 9. 1615-1616: Cornhill, London

The ride from Blackwall to Cornhill in London was a half-day carriage ride. They rode in a chaise, a horse-drawn carriage having two narrow, high wheels and a bench seat that could accommodate two people comfortably. "I heard of people to the west of my home who ride horses," Squanto told Slany, "and I saw men riding horses in Spain - but this is a first for me, seeing a horse pulling a carriage

Both men found the ride to be bumpy and uncomfortable. The road was just wide enough for one cart. When another cart came in the opposite direction, each driver needed to pull to one side to pass safely. At one point in their journey, a larger four-wheeled cart forced Slany's smaller cart further off the road. "Insolent manure cart drivers!" fumed Slany. "They know we have to get out of the way of their stinky loads!"

Squanto was aware that virtually everyone they met stared at him. He knew he was different from English people in many ways. Squanto also knew that Slany recognized his differences. "People will stare at you just because you're different from what they are used to seeing," Slany warned Squanto. "You're taller than most Englishmen, your skin is brown, you have no beard, your hair is long and straight, and when they hear you talk, they'll know you're not from England."

The two had talked about Squanto's differences. Had Squanto continued to dress as was usual for him in New England, wearing only a cloth around his loins, he would have created even more of a sensation. With Raleigh's and Slany's help, his attire now reflected English custom. The knee-length trousers, stockings, boots, linen shirt, and jacket all felt uncomfortable, but they helped him fit more readily into English society. Squanto was grateful for Slany's acceptance of his differences. Slany was patient in helping him master the English language, and in explaining the many new things Squanto experienced.

Squanto was impressed with the houses he saw in England. Most were built of stone and were rectangular or square. "Our homes are very different from these stone, houses," he remarked to Slany. "Ours are made of white cedar branches tied together with walnut bark."

"How do you keep warm in such houses?" asked Slany.

"We cover winter houses inside and outside with furs to keep out the snow and wind," responded Squanto. "Winter houses are further away from the ocean. Our summer houses are nearer the ocean. They don't have to be so warm, so we often use thatched reeds for a covering rather than furs."

The stone houses Squanto saw in England had chimneys to carry smoke from cooking or heating fires. Squanto asked about the small openings in the walls.

"Those openings are windows," said Slany. "We now put a clear material, glass, in them, but it breaks quite easily. The glass helps keep out the wind and rain, and at the same time, lets in light."

Squanto was in awe of the large buildings he saw as they came closer to London. They were made of wood and stone. "My people would think I have a wild imagination if I ever told them about the size of these buildings," Squanto said with a laugh. He knew his friends and family could hardly imagine the mass and strength of such structures.

"You say your home is in Cornhill," Squanto said to Slany. "Yes, Cornhill is an old part of London," responded Slany. "Many years ago, people sold corn there, so that is where the name came from."

"We grow corn," said Squanto. "In fact, my people grow more corn, squash, and beans than we need. The extra we use in trade with other bands where crops are less plentiful."

Slany had already considered Squanto's future usefulness to English traders and settlers because of his knowledge of the land and his ability to speak both English and Native American languages. Squanto's comments about winter and summer housing and growing corn, squash, and beans underscored for Slany the value Squanto could be to help colonists become self-sustaining.

Before arriving at Slany's home on Cornhill Street, they stopped to view the nearby Church of St. Michaels.

"I would like to look inside," said Squanto.

"Yes, come with me," responded Slany.

The two strolled slowly, Squanto taking in the height of the tower and the beauty of the structure. He noticed the evenly cut stones and timbers, the massive wood doors, and large windows. As the door swung open, Squanto's mouth dropped open. He was speechless as he took in the magnificent interior. The inside of St. Michaels was bathed in colors from afternoon sunlight that streamed through colored glass windows. Two rows of benches were on either side of a center aisle, which led to a table with beautiful ornaments. A large painting hung in the middle of the front wall. The ceiling was higher than he thought possible. It too was colorful. Squanto felt almost overwhelmed with wonder at the splendor, skills, and wealth the building represented.

A man dressed in black robes walked slowly toward them. "It's good to see you, Master Slany," he said, "and your friend as well!"

"Reverend Ashbold, it's good to be back in Cornhill, and I'm glad to see you as well," said Slany. "I would like you to meet my friend Squanto. He is from the New World and will be staying with me at my home."

"I'm so glad to meet you, Squanto," said Reverend Ashbold. "Welcome to St. Michaels."

"Thank you," Squanto responded. "Your building is beautiful. How will I ever describe it to my people?"

"Squanto," said the Rector, "Simply tell your people you saw a building whose purpose is to reflect the beauty of our Creator. The windows, the cross, the goblets, and trays – they all help tell the story of our Creator's love, and we use these things to celebrate His goodness to us."

Squanto drank in the striking beauty of the light within St. Michaels as the late afternoon sunlight continued to stream through the colored glass on the west side of the building. The metal goblets and silver trays, which he had never seen before, seemed almost to be aflame in the light. "I've seen that same shape hanging on the necks of some of the ship captains I met," he said, pointing to a cross.

"We must go before the sun sets," said Slany. He knew he was interrupting Squanto's thoughts, but he wanted to get to his home – a short distance from the church - before dark. They arrived as the sun was setting.

Chapter 10. 1618: Shakespeare, King James, and John Tilley

From the time Slany and Squanto met, Slany included Squanto in virtually all he did. In part, he did so because he enjoyed Squanto's company. He found Squanto to be intelligent, socially outgoing, eager to learn, and with a positive disposition. But Slany's motivation for including Squanto was very much driven by his vision of Squanto serving as an onsite interpreter and guide for employees of his company in the New World. Ship captains, colony governors, and settlers would all benefit from Squanto's proficiency with languages and his knowledge and skills of Native American ways. His expertise would provide a much shorter path to profits by helping establish settlements and trade that would otherwise develop more slowly.

For his part, Squanto was grateful that Slany treated him as an equal. He ate with Slany and went everywhere Slany went. Slany introduced Squanto to each person they met. While Batista had generally been kind to him, Squanto knew that in Spain, he was very much a slave. His movement in Malaga was limited to his work and living area. His only option was to work as Batista directed.

"At the right time, I want to send you to work with our Company in Newfoundland," Slany told Squanto. "We need your expertise there."

Slany's plan filled Squanto with hope. He could not help but wonder if his work and travel might mean he could reunite with his own people in Patuxet again. "When might that time come?" he asked himself.

In the spring of 1618, Slany told Squanto about a play that was to be held to honor the memory of an important Englishman, William Shakespeare, who had died two years earlier. One of Shakespeare's plays was to be performed in London at the newly reconstructed Globe Theater. The original Globe Theater had been destroyed by fire in 1613, and the new theater had recently been completed.

"I am taking you to a play, Squanto," said Slany. "I want you to see another part of our English culture. Remember when you told me how you and your friends acted out what you saw and heard from English sailors? At the play, you will see people acting out a story imagined by a man whose name is Shakespeare." Squanto looked forward to the adventure.

The Globe Theater was across the Thames River. They boarded a carriage in Cornhill in midmorning, traveled down Gracechurch Street and across the London Bridge. "The play will start just after high noon," Slany told Squanto. "The start time allows people to view the play in the day time, and everyone can return to their homes before dark." Slany and Squanto reached the theater ahead of most attendees, and their early arrival gave them time for a brief tour.

The new Globe Theater was a three-story, open-air structure about 100 feet in diameter. Three levels of seating surrounded an area open to the sky. The stage was rectangular and raised about shoulder high above the ground. Between the stage and raised seating was an area for people to stand.

When he had initially arrived back in England with Squanto, Slany had communicated to King James about Squanto being with him. He knew of the King's fascination with 'savages' from across the ocean. A year earlier, the king had invited Pocahontas and her husband, John Rolfe, to an elaborate party at Whitehall Palace during their visit to England. Slany was also quite aware that King James viewed lands claimed by sailors in his name as his, as did his predecessor, Queen Elisabeth. Both sovereigns granted charters to English companies to settle the territory, one of those charters being his own Company of Adventurers and Planters of London.

Slany chose this occasion to let King James know that Squanto would be with him at the Globe Theater and that it would be an opportune time for the king to meet a native from New England. Unsure of whether the king might come to the theater, Slany said nothing to Squanto.

The two toured the theater. Squanto smiled as they stood at ground level in front of the stage. "I know what orange peels are now," he said, pointing to remnants still in the dust. "And the shells are from hazelnuts. "We have those trees at my home in Patuxet!" Behind them and to each side, they looked up at permanent seating.

After taking in the interior of the theater, the two went back out through the main entrance. Slany saw palace guards strategically placed and immediately recognized that the King would be in attendance. He stopped near one of the guards and identified himself. "I am Master John Slany. With me today is a native from the New World. I need you to get word to the King that the native is waiting for him with me at the theater."

The guard rode briskly to meet the King and conveyed the information. "Return immediately to the theater," commanded the King. "Tell Master Slany and his friend to wait for me at the Royal Entrance at the side of the theater."

When the guard reported the King's command to Slany, Slany was elated. He reached up to put his hand on Squanto's shoulder and said with a smile, "Today, my good man, you will meet our King." Slany's excitement was contagious, and Squanto was filled with anticipation, delighted he would finally meet the king he had heard so much about. He walked with Slany to the royal entrance. Within minutes, the lead group of the King's entourage arrived with the King not far behind. King James rode a large white horse. His hands held the saddle horn rather than the reins. Today's journey was short, and for such rides, he relied on grooms running along either side to guide his horse. However, the horse was spirited, and for a moment before the horse stopped for the King to dismount, Squanto thought the King might fall off.

King James approached, and Slany bowed, "Your Majesty, Sir." I am pleased to bring a representative from your new realm across the vast ocean. This is Squanto."

"Thank you, Master Slany," replied the King. "I am grateful for your service."

"It is an honor to serve you, Your Majesty," responded Slany.

The King looked directly at Squanto, "Welcome, Squanto. You are a part of the New World I have heard so much about. My sailing captains have told me much about the beauty and wealth of the land. I am pleased to hear that you will work with Master Slany."

"I am glad to meet you, King James," responded Squanto in almost perfect English. "Your sailing captains told me much about you - as has Master Slany. You are right. The land of my home is large, beautiful, and rich in many ways."

"I would be pleased to have you and Master Slany join me to watch the play this afternoon," said the King. "Please accompany me to the royal box."

"We are honored to do so," replied Slany.

The King, Slany, and Squanto entered the theater and sat in the royal box. As the theater filled, all eyes turned toward the strange grouping. How amazing to see a king and what many thought, a savage, seated side by side. Could anyone have imagined a more improbable connection?!

One of those in the audience who saw the King and savage in the royal box was John Tilley, Elisabeth's father. In an improbable twist of circumstances, John attended the play at the urging of his friend and solicitor, George Smyth. John had returned on a secretive trip to England, to seek George's help in disposing of family assets. John's life for the last several years had been in Holland with other Separatists; but circumstances in Holland were changing, and the Separatists there were actively exploring the possibility of establishing their own plantation north of Jamestown in Virginia. To help finance such a journey, all assets in England needed to be sold.

Chapter 11. At *the Tempest*

George Smyth had been good friends with John and Joan Tilley back in their days in Henlow. George was now a solicitor in London. While he was not himself a Separatist, George was sympathetic toward their views and rationale for leaving the Anglican Church. Because of his longtime friendship with the Tilley family and the passion he felt about individual rights, George agreed to shelter John during John's visit to England, and help him with the sale of family property north of London. "I'm sure you understand what a big risk this is for me, John," George had said. "but your cause has my sympathies. I'll do what I can to help."

During the time John was back in England, George had planned to take his wife, Isabel, to Shakespeare's play, *The Tempest*; however, Isabel had been called away from London to an uncle's home in Henlow. Her cousin, Mary, was ill, and the family had requested Isabel's help to provide short term care. Since John Tilley was staying at the Smyth home, George invited John to attend the play with him in place of Isabel. "Shakespeare's plays are carnal, George," John said. "How can such performances encourage our spiritual growth?"

But George argued, "Look beyond the theater, John, and some of Shakespeare's other plays. There are redeeming themes in this performance. You'll see a king lose his kingdom, and before retaliating, he learns that forgiveness is more important than vengeance." At George's urging, John finally agreed to go.

"No one will recognize you there, John," George said. "You've been away from England for ten years. And the Theater is at least a full day's journey from where you used to live. No one from Henlow will be there."

Now from his seat in the theater, John gazed with mixed emotions at the King and the savage who sat beside him in the royal box. He looked with disdain at the King, whose authority over church worship he rejected. John breathed a brief prayer of forgiveness for his thoughts. After all, though he believed the King's power over how to worship was very wrong – as well as his jailing or putting to death those who disagreed with him - the King was still one of God's children. "I must pray for him," John thought as he remembered biblical exhortations to pray for leaders - and for enemies. God could do the impossible.

On the other hand, John could not help but look with a sense of wonder at the savage who sat beside the King. "Is it possible he is a killer?" John thought to himself. While at the University of Leiden with William Brewster last year, he and William read a report that told of natives attacking and killing English sailors. What if we were to sail to America? Would it be possible to live in peace with these people? He took in the brown skin; the straight, shoulder-length, black hair; the high cheekbones. Dare he hope his community of Separatists would find friendship among such people? Yes! And even more, John breathed a prayer that even beyond a peaceful relationship, the Native Americans might join with the Separatists in the worship of their Creator.

John could not yet know of the epic journey that lay ahead, nor of the hardships and tragedies his small band of Separatists would face, nor could he begin to imagine that the Native American sitting beside King James would not only befriend the Separatists but would share the knowledge and skills that would allow a small group of survivors – including his daughter Elisabeth - to survive after a dreadful beginning in America.

Chapter 12. Summer 1618: Squanto leaves England

In the early summer of 1618, John Slany received a communication from Governor John Mason who led the onsite operations for the Company of Merchant Adventurers at Cuper's Cove. The settlement was in Conception Bay on the Avalon Peninsula of Newfoundland. The site, now known as Cupids, had been established eight years earlier by John Guy, a member of the Company, to support and supply English fishermen.

"This area around Cuper's Cove can supply fishermen, but beyond that, the location has limited possibilities," Governor Mason wrote. "There is a need to look for settings where traders and colonists can establish ties with natives and build permanent footholds in the New World. Fish are plentiful in this area of Cuper's Cove," continued the Governor, "but furs are limited – and that is where profits are to be made." He added, "The land in this area is not well suited for crops. I need your support in looking for more suitable sites further west."

Slany immediately recognized that Squanto would be the ideal fit to meet Governor Mason's needs. It was time to implement the next stage of his plan. Squanto would leave England and fulfill his destiny back in the New World. Squanto's ability to communicate clearly with other Native Americans and with the English, his knowledge of the land, and his insights into both cultures would surely provide a fast track to profits for the Company and a more solid start for settlements.

Master Slany explained clearly to Squanto what he expected: "I need you to assist Captain John Mason at the Cuper's Cove settlement in Newfoundland about favorable areas for English settlement, where and how agriculture endeavors can succeed, and where fur trading is profitable. Governor Mason will need you to serve as an interpreter with other Native Americans you meet in your travels with him."

Squanto was thrilled with the news. "I will gladly work with Governor Mason in Newfoundland," Squanto said. It meant he would be an important step closer to his home. In July of 1618, Squanto found himself on another ship, crossing the ocean once more.

Chapter 13. Squanto in Newfoundland

During his growing up years, Squanto learned to adapt to different personalities in different settings. It helped that he had a high level of interpersonal intelligence. He knew how to get along with others, understand and anticipate their needs, and communicate clearly. Doing so made life much more pleasant. His adaptability and interpersonal skills suited him well to travel with Samoset, and connect with other bands of Native Americans. Squanto was able to build trust and acceptance with others.

His capacity to adapt to various situations and interact with diverse personalities worked well for him in England. Upon arriving in Cuper's Cove, the same skills aided the development of his relationship with Governor Mason. When the Governor asked Squanto how fur trading could be enhanced, Squanto was quick to point, "I lived in an area to the south-west of here where furs are bountiful, and trade is welcomed. I can guide you there."

"I would like you to dine with me this evening to talk further on the matter," the Governor said. High on the Governor's agenda of dinner time conversation was asking Squanto to expand on his ideas about where fur trading would be most profitable.

"The lands that Captain Smith named, New England, are ideal for the fur trade," Squanto told him. "I grew up in that area. Many animals provide us with fur there. We also grow corn, squash, and beans," he said. "When I lived there, we grew more food than we needed, and we traded with our neighbors to the north who sometimes have more furs than corn."

He told Governor Mason of his meeting in England with Sir Walter Raleigh. "He knew of lands to the south and west of here," Squanto told him. "His settlers found land that was good for farming in Virginia."

"I can guide you to where you want to go," Squanto said with confidence, "I know the people and the language. I can show you firsthand the most advantageous locations for settlement. I have many contacts who would welcome your trade."

While his advice to Governor Mason about agriculture and the fur trade was accurate, Squanto also had his own agenda: Deep down, he wanted to return to his home and family in Patuxet - in the area Governor Mason knew as New England. But there was a possibility of more. The English needed his connections with his people, and his own people could benefit from trade with the English. He, Squanto, could be the link. Both parties would need him – and he would control communication.

Governor Mason was impressed with Squanto's command of the English language, his evident first-hand knowledge of Sir Walter Raleigh, and his understanding of the New England lands Captain Smith had named and where Squanto had lived. The next day the Governor summoned one of his most trusted Captains, Thomas Dermer, and together with Squanto, they began planning and preparing for an excursion to New England.

Sailing trips out of Cuper's Cove in 1619 had weather risks, but what concerned ship captains even more, was the possibility of pirates. Governor Mason had fortified the colony at Cuper's Cove against attacks from pirates.

"One of the first requirements for our venture to New England is a fast ship," he told Dermer. Governor Mason was most concerned about one pirate in particular, Peter Easton. "He used to work for Queen Elizabeth as part of her navy," Mason said. "When James became king, he signed a peace treaty with Spain and stopped paying Easton in order to save money. So Easton just plain turned to piracy. That scoundrel is now one of the most successful pirates on the high seas. He plunders ships from here to the Mediterranean no matter what their country of origin: France, Spain, Portugal, Holland, and – get this - even English ships!"

"Then we certainly need a ship as fast or faster than his," Dermer said. "I believe we have one in port here that will work."

"It's a chance we must take," responded the Governor. "Let me know by this time tomorrow what men and provisions you need," Mason said to Dermer.

"Squanto, you will go with Captain Dermer and guide him to the area you know in New England."

It took ten days to prepare for the expedition. Provisions were assembled and the ship readied. Dermer, Squanto, and crew set sail out of Cuper's Cove in May of 1619, bound for the coast of New England.

Chapter 14. An Unexpected Welcome

Fortunately for Captain Dermer and crew, they saw no sign of the pirate, Easton.

Squanto felt the excitement grow within him as the New England coast came into view. The sun had been up for about three hours, and the day was bright and beautiful. Soon, he was sure, he would reunite with his Patuxet family. He guided Captain Dermer into the bay offshore from his Patuxet home. He saw no one on the land, but that was not unusual. He had been taught from childhood to be wary of any visitors – especially English or French sailors who came in their large 'floating islands.' He felt sure there were several sets of eyes watching from the forests. No doubt the people of his village and even neighboring communities had been alerted about the approaching vessel.

Captain Dermer dropped anchor in Plymouth Harbor about a mile offshore. The shallowness of the bay prevented a closer approach. He commanded that a shallop be lowered. Then he and Squanto and 14 sailors boarded the small craft and rowed to shore. Shortly after mid-day, they stepped ashore near Squanto's home of Patuxet. Squanto led the group toward his village; however, there was an unusual quietness. Squanto sensed that something was wrong.

The corn and squash fields were cleared and ready for planting. By this time in late spring, he would have expected to see new growth. And where were the wetu? "Have my people moved?" he wondered.

Looking closer, he made a gruesome discovery. Bones and skulls of people were scattered across the ground. Nearby he saw evidence of many shallow graves. Slowly a picture of what happened began to emerge. A debilitating sickness must have descended upon his people and spread rapidly. Those who died first were buried. When the epidemic engulfed everyone in the community and more died, the living could not keep up with the burials – until those who died last remained on the surface. Squanto had once happened upon such a disastrous scene on a journey with Samoset.

"Did any survive?" he wondered. Looking further, he recognized the charred remains of wetu. Someone had burned the homes to halt the spread of disease. He looked around until he found what might have been the charred remains where his mother, father, and two sisters lived.

Emotion overtook him. At first, he sobbed gently. Then the extent of death and loss began to sink in. If any in his community had survived the sickness, the bones of those remaining would not scattered on the surface for crows, hawks or other scavengers. They would have been buried. A visceral scream came from within Squanto. He fell to the ground among the bones, heaving with emotion.

Captain Dermer and the men with him felt a chill as they heard Squanto scream. Each of the men knelt with heads bowed. What can one say to comfort a man whose whole village has died – family, friends, acquaintances?

Later in the day, Captain Dermer put his arm around Squanto and directed him back to the shallop. "We'll return to our ship for the night," he told Squanto. Squanto did not resist, and almost in a trance, sat quietly as the sailors rowed back to the ship.

Captain Dermer waited three days before talking further to Squanto. During that time, Squanto took no nourishment other than water. Early on the morning of the fourth day, Captain Dermer brought a breakfast of fresh fried fish to Squanto and said, "You need some sustenance, my friend. Let's return to shore in the shallop to see whether neighboring villages know what happened to your people." The food strengthened

Squanto, and along with Dermer's encouragement, his spirits lifted. Squanto knew that other bands of Native Americans lived within two day's journey. Perhaps they could tell him more of what happened at his village.

"Yes, let's go ashore, Captain," responded Squanto.

Within the hour a shallop was lowered, and the same 14 sailors, accompanied by Captain Dermer and Squanto, rowed the mile to shore.

Chapter 15. From Company Advisor to Captive

Squanto's plan was to begin walking southwest toward the village of Sowams where the Pokanoket band lived. He knew that Massasoit, leader of the Pokanokets and head of the Wampanoag Nation, lived there. If anyone knew what had happened to his people, it would be Massasoit. Squanto also knew that Massasoit would be open to trade. In the past, he had traded furs with English sailors for metal tools, including axes and hoes. For information and business, Massasoit would be the place to start.

The group walked less than a mile from where they had beached the shallop when they were surprised by a band of thirty Pokanoket warriors, all of whose faces were painted: some red, others black, and still others yellow or white. All were armed with bows and arrows. The warriors appeared suddenly at the edge of the tree line on a slight rise about 50 yards away. Whether it was the unexpectedness of their appearance, their fearsome look, or both, several sailors were frightened and quickly fired their rifles, killing two warriors.

"No!" Shouted Squanto, horrified at the sudden turn of events. He could not believe what just happened, but he knew what would occur next. The Pokanoket warriors descended upon Dermer's party at full speed with fearful screams, firing arrows and brandishing tomahawks. Several arrows found their mark. The sailors who were still standing attempted to reload their rifles, but the process took too long. They quickly saw the need for a hasty retreat toward the shallop. However, Pokanoket warriors were quicker and were brutally efficient with their tomahawks. Only Dermer and three wounded sailors escaped death by reaching the shallop, pushing it into the ocean, and rowing for their lives.

The Pokanokets recognized Squanto as Native American and therefore did not kill him. But because he was with the English sailors, they took him captive to Sowams to meet Chief Massasoit.

Massasoit listened at length to Squanto's astonishing story. "I heard of the treachery of the English captain and your kidnapping," said Massasoit. "And we knew of the tragedy in your village. When we saw that everyone died, my men burned the wetu there to prevent the spread of sickness."

Massasoit felt empathy for Squanto's loss of family. However, Squanto had arrived in the company of English sailors who killed two of his own warriors, and he was uncertain as to whether Squanto could be trusted. He kept Squanto captive in Sowams for two years until the spring of 1621, when Squanto's old friend Samoset appealed to Massasoit saying, "We need Squanto's skills with English to better learn the intentions of the new English settlers."

PART III. ELISABETH'S STORY

Chapter 16. Escape from England

In 1614, during her seventh spring, Elisabeth and her parents, John and Joan Tilley, left Henlow on a secretive trip to Gravesend on the south side of the Thames River in southwest England. Their purpose was to board a small ship that would take them to Holland to join a group of Separatists who had left England several years earlier. Both parents were outwardly calm – partly because of their firm belief that God would protect them, but also because they did not want Elisabeth to be fearful. Elisabeth had heard some of the hushed conversations between her parents about the risks of leaving England, but she felt excited about the travel and the new experiences and adventure that lay ahead.

The Tilleys had good reason to be concerned about their travel. They knew it was illegal to leave England for the purpose of religious freedom. A group of about 40 Separatist acquaintances had left Gainsborough England without being noticed by authorities in the summer of 1607.

Later that same year, friends from Scrooby were not so fortunate. They traveled to Scotia Creek near Boston in Lincolnshire County, eastern England where they contracted with a sailing captain for passage to Holland. "The captain was a scoundrel," a friend later told Joan Tilley. "Before we boarded the ship, the captain alerted the Boston sheriff. Just as we started to load our things, we were all arrested and taken to prison. Our belongings were seized. The jail was so crowded that it was not practical for the sheriff to keep us all. He released women and children within a few days, and some of our men were also let go. But our elders were held in prison for over three months."

Other acquaintances of the Tilleys also tried to escape England in 1607. John attended the initial planning sessions and knew the group decided to leave England through Immingham, rather than Boston. John's brother, Edward, traveled with one family to Immingham simply to help in the moving process. On his return, he told a harrowing story.

"The captain of the ship stationed a sailor to keep watch for any unusual police or soldier activity. After we finished loading everyone's belongings on board ship, the sailor on watch alerted the captain of a military detachment advancing toward the harbor. The captain was afraid his ship might be seized, and that he would face jail or a fine – so he ordered his crew to set sail immediately. It was horrible! The men on board protested loudly because their women and children had not yet boarded. Sailors untied the lines, raised the gangplank, and cast off from the dock. The women and children were still at the church awaiting word to leave their sanctuary to board the ship. Fortunately, I was not on board when the ship cast off. I went back to the church to let the women know what had transpired."

"Providentially," Edward continued, "the Rector at the church was sympathetic enough to our cause that he allowed the women and children to stay at the church until the ship that took their men returned. We can only hope they all reunited successfully in Holland."

The Separatists learned in these early attempts to leave England in small groups. When John and Joan Tilley determined it was time for them to leave England to join other Separatists in Holland, they became one of these small groups.

In early May of 1614, two Tilley families traveled together. The group included Elisabeth's parents, John and Joan; her father's brother, Edward, his wife, Agnes; and Agnes' teenaged brother, Robert Cooper. They traveled from Henlow to the town of Tilbury on the banks of the Thames.

During the journey, the two families encountered a group of six children begging on the outskirts of a village. "Do they not have a home, Father?" asked Elisabeth.

"It's possible their parents died," he responded. "They probably live in that building over there," he said, pointing to a nearby structure. "It's called a house of correction. Children go to a place like that when their parents die, and no one else wants to look after them. Sometimes poor people who have no income or don't have their own home must live in a place like that."

"I feel so sorry for those children!" Elisabeth said. I wish we could take them with us! They look so sad."

Her father put his hand on her shoulder as they walked on. "I feel sorry for them, too," he said, "but we just can't do anything for them right now. We have many dangers and uncertainties of our own to face in the days ahead."

Upon arriving at Tilbury, they boarded a ferry to cross the Thames to Gravesend. There the families overnighted at St. George's Church where a compassionate but nervous Rector, Thomas Argyle, allowed them to stay. "There are many visitors in town, and I'm praying you won't be noticed," he said. "King James and Prince Charles are coming to Gravesend in a few days to meet the King of Denmark at the Ship's Inn. If all goes well, the sheriff and his men will be so focused on assisting the King's advance party, they won't have time to check on Church visitors."

The Church, at the foot of High Street, was a short distance from the harbor. In the morning, Elisabeth and her family boarded a small ship unnoticed by the sheriff. The ship they boarded was carrying broadcloth and other woolens on the five-day voyage to Delfshaven, Holland. From Delfshaven they would make their way to Leiden where English friends had already settled.

Chapter 17. Leiden

Separatists from the Anglican Church who left England for Holland found employment in two centers: Amsterdam and Leiden. Holland had the highest per capita income of any European country at that time, and the relative prosperity and larger population meant that jobs – though low-paying – were available. Elisabeth and her family settled in Leiden. About 40,000 people lived there - much larger than their hometown of Henlow. Housing was available near the University of Leiden. The Tilleys found a small, two-room cottage east of the University close to Pieterskerk, the largest and oldest cathedral in Holland.

Elisabeth's father found work almost immediately in a textile factory where he helped in the making of camlet, a relatively expensive fabric fashioned from camel or goat's hair. It was a relief to John to have a job that would feed his family. Elisabeth's mother was hired at the nearby van Zuytbroeck bakery.

The Separatists met twice a week to fellowship with one another and listen to sermons by Pastor John Robinson. They gathered at a chapel on the campus of the University of Leiden. Robinson's academic background at Cambridge University opened doors for him at the University, allowing him to interact with faculty and provide access to university facilities. He was active in the Theology Department, attending lectures by professors who held divergent views on topics in theology, and occasionally mediating their differences. The Rector Magnificus of the University, Rudolph Snellius, observed Robinson's critical thinking skills and appreciated them. He also respected Separatist, Thomas Brewer's excellence in English, and hired him to teach at the University. In keeping with the University's motto, *Bastion of Freedom*, Snellius offered the use of one of its chapels to Robinson. "Your group is welcome here at the University," he told Robinson. "Please extend an invitation to them to attend special lectures we hold here from time to time here at the University."

For the Separatist adults, meeting times with Pastor Robinson were serious occasions. They had risked their very lives and left possessions to come to Leiden to worship according to their conscience. Most knew friends who had died or were in English jails for worshiping outside the Anglican Church or for attempting to leave England. At times the meetings were emotional.

Elisabeth and other children looked forward to church gatherings as a time to meet friends - even though the services were long. Elisabeth thoroughly enjoyed interacting with Desire Minter and Mary Chilton. The girls often worked together to care for younger children during church services. Whenever time permitted, the girls had adventures together exploring the nearby University grounds or along the banks of Leiden's canals.

When Joan Tilley began work, she took Elisabeth with her each day to the bakery. The two had lunch together, and Joan felt relieved that Elisabeth was not alone at home. The bakery manager, Mrs. van Rijn, noticed Elisabeth and told Joan about the need for someone to help keep the floors clean. Believing it was better to have her daughter close by, Joan responded, "I'm sure my daughter could do that job."

"Let's give her a try," said Mrs. van Rijn. So not long before her eighth birthday, Elisabeth began work at the bakery.

The Tilley family needed everything they could earn to pay for food and rent. About a month after beginning work at the bakery, Joan learned from Mrs. van Rijn that her husband needed to hire a worker at his mill. John went to investigate and discovered that pay would be higher than at the textile factory where he currently worked. At the beginning of the next week, John Tilley began work at Harmen van

Rijn's mill.

Elisabeth enjoyed her time at the bakery. It was a hive of activity, and the owners were kind to her. Mrs. van Rijn noticed the excellence with which Elisabeth carried out her responsibility of keeping the floors clean. If flour, seeds, or breadcrumbs sat there very long, mice – or worse yet, rats - soon found out and came for a feast. Elisabeth's helpers were two cats. They were the bakery's official rodent patrol. Elisabeth and the cats thoroughly enjoyed one another's company. The cats seemed to alternate between sleeping, rubbing against her as if asking to be petted, and hunting for mice or rats. Elisabeth was amazed at how quickly the cats could go from what seemed like deep sleep to full-blown mouse attack.

A few weeks after she started at the bakery, Elisabeth met the son of the woman who supervised her work, Mrs. van Rijn. His name was Rembrandt, a boy that Elisabeth later learned was exactly one year older than she. Rembrandt went to Latin School. "We hope he will attend the University of Leiden, in a few years," his mother told Elisabeth's mother. "The university will give him a much greater opportunity for success in business," she added.

As Elisabeth was to find out, Rembrandt was highly intelligent and did well at school. However, his heart was not in academic pursuits. He had a very keen sense of observation. His passion was drawing and painting.

The day that Elisabeth and Rembrandt met, he had come to the bakery directly from school. "I'm so hungry, and the bread smells so good," he told his mother. She gave him a chunk of freshly baked bread. He was enjoying the first morsel when he saw Elisabeth sweeping the floor behind a counter. He immediately came to see who she was. "And who are you?" he asked. Elisabeth did not understand the words Rembrandt spoke but guessed he was asking who she was. She pointed to herself and said, "I'm Elisabeth."

Though they spoke different languages, the children sensed an immediate connection with one another. Rembrandt offered some of his bread to Elisabeth. She was grateful and broke off a chunk. From that day forward, Rembrandt came daily to the bakery after school. He and Elisabeth became firm friends.

As time passed, Elisabeth's mother took notice and was grateful that Rembrandt was so kind to Elisabeth. Joan Tilley observed at supper one evening, "Each of us has a connection with the van Rijn family: John works with Harmen, Elisabeth and I work with Harmen's wife, Neeltgen, at the bakery, and Elisabeth is also friends with Rembrandt."

While other children and even some grownups made fun of Elisabeth because she spoke very little Dutch, Rembrandt was much more sensitive. He communicated with her initially by making signs and then saying the Dutch words. Elisabeth learned quickly, and within weeks, the two carried on basic conversations.

In addition to sharing a bread treat with Elisabeth on each visit, Rembrandt helped with some of the floor cleaning duties, and together they tended the cats. With each visit, Elisabeth gained proficiency in communicating verbally in Dutch. Her parents noticed and had mixed feelings about her learning. On the one hand, they appreciated Elisabeth's ability to converse in Dutch. She could go with them to the market and help in bargaining with vendors. On the other hand, a seed of concern began to grow. Would their daughter lose her English sensibilities and customs, or more importantly, was she being drawn to relationships and friendships that might take her from their Separatist church?

As Elisabeth's and Rembrandt's conversations in Dutch became more fluent, Elisabeth asked Rembrandt, "What do you learn at Latin School?"

"I'll bring some of my school work to show you," he said. And the next day, Rembrandt brought a sample of his writing to show Elisabeth.

She was awed by how he was able to write on parchment and read to her the words he had written. "Do you think I could learn to do that, Rembrandt?" she asked. He laughed, and Elisabeth looked closely at him to see whether he was laughing *at* her. She soon realized his laugh was only because her question had surprised him. "Of course you can learn to read and write!" he exclaimed. "Girls can do that! My older sister, Lysbeth, helped me to read and write. Here, you draw the same letters I've drawn, but do it right underneath my writing." And so, Rembrandt not only helped Elisabeth learn to speak Dutch, but he also became her reading and writing teacher. Elisabeth was a keen student, soaking up the learning.

Both children loved to dream and talk with one another about their aspirations. Elisabeth imagined living in a country house like some she saw while traveling in England. "It would have to be large enough to care for children who needed a home," she announced, "I met six children in England who needed a home, and I'm sure there are many others just like them. We would all stay together, and we would look after cats and dogs and sheep and chickens."

Rembrandt dreamed of drawing and painting. "I want to be an artist," he said. "At Latin School, the teachers expect us to learn logic, but I need more. The headmaster told us recently of a fascinating thing in natural philosophy. When he said it, I felt a big 'Yes' inside," said Rembrandt, pointing to his heart. "The headmaster told us something St. Augustine said that went like, 'Truth should be expressed with beauty, love, and hope.' It helped me understand why I like to draw so much. I want to draw what I see and capture it beautifully. I need that kind of creativity." Rembrandt loved to observe people, and Elisabeth was amazed at how accurately he sketched what he saw. She had watched him sketch a bakery worker, make a wonderfully accurate representation of the cats, and even draw a beautiful illustration of a boat they saw on the Rhine River.

"Do you think you could draw a picture of me sometime?" she asked him. He looked at her thoughtfully for a few moments, taking in her brown eyes, heart-shaped face, and light brown hair. A smile broke across his face, and he responded, "Yes, I will sketch a picture of you…and someday I will paint a beautiful picture of you."

Elisabeth could tell by Rembrandt's careful response that it was not an idle promise.

Chapter 18. Leiden Thanksgiving

Over their six years in Leiden, the Tilley family grew close to the van Rijn family. The van Rijn's hosted the Tilley's on several occasions for dinner. Elisabeth looked forward to the visits because so much was always happening in the van Rijn home. She enjoyed the interaction with Rembrandt's older brothers and sisters, especially with Lysbeth, who treated Elisabeth like a younger sister she never had.

On October 3rd, 1619, Elisabeth and her parents attended a dinner at the van Rijn home. Three things happened that evening that Elisabeth never forgot.

The first occurred during the walk to the van Rijn home with her parents. As they passed a construction site, Mr. Tilley stopped for a moment and said to Elisabeth, "Do you see that line of string suspended from the cross members at the corner of the building?"

Elisabeth noticed the line and the stone tied at the bottom to keep the line taut. "Yes, Father, I see it," she said. "Why do they need that?"

"That's called a plumb line, Dear. It lets the builders know what is exactly vertical – exactly straight up and down. Without a plumb line, the walls might not be straight – and if the walls of the building were not vertical, they could collapse on the people inside."

"That would be terrible," said Elisabeth.

They were silent for a few moments, and then Mr. Tilley said, "Elisabeth, you may never build a house, but I want you always to remember there is a plumb line in life. It's called love. We can measure actions and words by how they reflect love. If we truly love our Creator, ourselves, and others, the plumb line of love will guide us to be good friends and to make wise choices about relationships."

Elisabeth did not say anything, but looked up at her father, smiled, and squeezed his hand. She did not know it at the time, but in a few short years, her father would be taken from her. She would remember this moment of closeness and the principle her father conveyed to her many times throughout her life.

The second thing that Elisabeth never forgot was the kindness of Rembrandt's older sister, Lysbeth. Prior to sitting down for dinner, Lysbeth took Elisabeth into her room. The two sorted through clothing in Lysbeth's dresser and closet. "Elisabeth, here's a red dress I used to wear," said Lysbeth. "It's too small for me now, but I think it could be just right for you."

Elisabeth tried on the dress, and it was close to a perfect fit. "It's beautiful, Lysbeth," said Elisabeth, running her hands over the luxurious cloth. Lysbeth was already looking for accessories to go with the dress. "Here, try on this hat," she said, placing it at a slight angle on Elisabeth's head. "Oh, you look adorable!" exclaimed Lysbeth. "Come, let's show our parents."

Elisabeth walked out to the dining room, feeling somewhat self-conscious. She was afraid her parents might disapprove and wondered if someone would make fun of her. But the reaction was not what she feared. Her parents and Mr. and Mrs. van Rijn all clapped their hands and exclaimed how beautiful she looked. Rembrandt did not say anything, but Elisabeth could tell by his intense look that he was taking in every detail.

"Keep the dress on for our supper," said Lysbeth, "and then you can wear it home." The dress was the most elegant clothing Elisabeth had ever worn. She removed the hat as the family prepared to sit down for dinner.

The dinner menu and what was celebrated was the third thing Elisabeth never forgot about the evening. Mr. van Rijn recounted the story before food was served. "October 3rd is our Thanksgiving Day here in Leiden," he said. "Each year on this day, we celebrate the liberation of our city from a siege by the Spanish army back in 1574. The siege was so long that half the population of Leiden died of starvation. It was a horrible time. Finally, our liberation army broke the siege. My parents survived that awful experience, but my grandparents did not." He paused briefly, and Elisabeth saw tears form in his eyes. He continued, "I was a young boy at the time. I remember the constant hunger, and finally the relief when our army came into the city. They brought herring, white bread, and cheese with them – enough for all of us to share. I don't remember how the food tasted, but I remember clearly how it made my tummy feel so much better. Now, each of these foods is part of our annual Thanksgiving meal."

Mrs. Van Rijn was seated to his right. He placed his hand on his wife's arm. "My wife uses variations of these three foods to make the most delicious Thanksgiving meal. I know you'll enjoy her dinner this evening." And they did.

As the Tilley's prepared to leave the van Rijn household later in the evening, Lysbeth helped Elisabeth put on the black hat. Rembrandt whispered to Elisabeth, "That's the dress and hat you'll be wearing when I do a painting of you!"

Just over twenty years later, in 1641, Rembrandt completed his famous painting, The Girl in a Picture Frame.

Chapter 19. A Visit to the University

During a lunch break at the mill one day, Harmen van Rijn told John Tilley about an upcoming event at the University of Leiden to which he was taking Rembrandt. "He has done well in Latin school, John, and I want him to attend the University next year. I think the visit will show young Rembrandt what wonderful learning the University will provide for him. I would like you to come with us and bring Elisabeth. She and Rembrandt are such good friends. Perhaps she will even encourage him to attend there. He spends so much time drawing and sketching that I think he forgets that the University is where his future must be. I'm certain that graduation from the University will take him places he hasn't yet imagined."

"I would love to come with you," said John, "and I know young Elisabeth will be very excited to join us."

"The lecture is scheduled for next week," Harmen said. "It is about the infinitely small and the infinitely large. The public are invited, and no doubt, some of your Separatist friends will attend. Our Dutch countrymen have designed a microscope that looks at things much smaller than we can see with our eyes, and they have also designed an instrument for looking at the stars, a telescope. Apparently, an Italian, Galileo Galilei, used a telescope to look at the heavens, and over the course of several nights, he claimed to see stars change places around the bright Jupiter. I think it will be interesting to hear reports about what he saw and what the professors at the University think he saw. I hope that the lecture and visit will interest my son enough to leave behind his fantasy about art and encourage him to focus on more meaningful learning.

Elisabeth was almost beyond excited to learn she would attend a lecture with her father at the University, joining Rembrandt and his father. She and her dad often sat outside at nighttime, looking at the heavens. She imagined different shapes and patterns the stars made and loved to see shooting stars flash across the sky. Besides, the lecture would also be an opportunity to see the inside of buildings at the University. She had only been inside the Chapel to attend church services. 'What were those other buildings like?' she had often thought. "What did people do there?" Now she would find out.

Elisabeth wore the red dress given her by Rembrandt's sister Lysbeth when she and her father went to meet Mr. van Rijn and Rembrandt in the late afternoon. She wanted to look her best. The lecture was scheduled such that discussion could take place prior to sunset. When they entered the University lecture hall, Elisabeth was captivated with its beauty. The grand paintings, beautiful woodwork, and massive doors set the room apart as important and special.

A low murmur spread throughout the room as people visited with one another before the lecture. The van Rijns and Tilleys found four seats together. She noticed her father nod to Pastor John Robinson and Mr. Brewster, who were a few rows closer to the front.

As Elisabeth looked around, she felt a bit self-conscious. "I think I'm the only girl here," she whispered to her father. Her father looked around and whispered back, "I think you're right!" She looked at her father with a nervous smile and felt comforted by his arm around her shoulder. Elisabeth was excited to be here with him and grateful to Mr. van Rijn for inviting her to be with them. Her father leaned over and whispered, "Listen carefully, my dear. You may have to interpret for me what the professors say tonight. I understand some of their language, but not nearly as well as you do." Elisabeth smiled up at her father.

The most exhilarating part of the evening for Elisabeth came when the lectures were over, and the crowd went outside. It was dusk with lingering sunlight, but Jupiter was already bright in the evening sky.

The men had lined up for an opportunity to look through the telescope at Jupiter and its four stars – moons, Galileo had called them because they were not always in the same location in relation to the much larger and brighter Jupiter. Elisabeth did not expect to be able to look through the telescope. All those present were men. A few boys Rembrandt's age were there with fathers. But when the time came for the van Rijns and her father to look through the telescope, the supervising professor noticed Elisabeth. "Why, young lady, I believe you are the only girl here tonight. Would you like to look through the telescope?" Elisabeth was so shocked at his offer that she could only look up at him and smile.

"Oh, yes, she would love to see Jupiter!" blurted Rembrandt, nudging her forward. The professor moved a stool close to the base of the telescope and helped Elisabeth up. He leaned in to check that Jupiter was still within the scope of vision, then said, "Close one eye and look through the lens with your other eye." She saw the brightest point of light, Jupiter. Then, unmistakably, she noticed the three small dots of light on one side. On the other side was one additional dot of light. She recalled the lecturer saying, "We know the dots of light are moons that revolve around Jupiter because sometimes all four are on one side; sometimes two are on one side, and two on the other side; and sometimes three are on one side and one on the other side." Her father gently lifted her down from the stool, and others took their turn viewing.

Elisabeth was speechless. Her mother would not believe Elisabeth had looked through a telescope. Girls were not expected to read or write – never mind engage in cutting-edge science. But her father was there. His hand had been on her shoulder when she looked through the telescope. And he too had looked through the telescope and knew what she saw! Her mother would have to believe her. And what would her friends Mary Chilton and Desire Minter think? She couldn't wait to tell them. She couldn't stop smiling because she – a girl – had seen a new world. It was another experience she would remember for the rest of her life.

Chapter 20. Leaving Leiden

While Elisabeth's attachment to life in Leiden was growing, she knew her parents and others in the Separatist Church felt troubled about how she and other young people in the congregation were becoming more Dutch than English. Pastor John Robinson and the elders warned parents about losing their children to a permissive Dutch culture. Elisabeth and other Separatist children had become quite fluent in Dutch and had formed strong friendships with other Dutch children. Indeed, some of the older Separatist children had already married into Dutch families.

Concern about their children was one of several factors that prompted Separatist parents to explore options for leaving Holland. In addition to worrying about seeing their children embrace Dutch culture, they also felt apprehension about the growing possibility of war with Catholic Spain. What if Holland were to again come under Catholic domination? In addition, pressure was mounting from the English ambassador to Holland for Dutch authorities to arrest William Brewster and Thomas Brewer. King James was furious about pamphlets the men printed at their press in Leiden and then smuggled into England. The King was aggressively hostile, calling such challenges to the Church of England seditious. He created political pressure on Dutch authorities, seeking the arrest and extradition of the men.

If only they could find a place where their families could worship without external pressures! Their desire for freedom of worship was very real. They knew a return to England was out of the question because King James still actively opposed them. Besides, most of the Separatist families had sold their property in England. Even if England were an option, going back would mean a whole new beginning. Talk and planning turned toward a more radical move: establishing a plantation in America – perhaps north of Jamestown, Virginia, where the distance across the ocean would make interference from the English king and his church minimal. In 1611, King James had granted a charter to the Virginia Company to farm or settle land 200 miles to the north and 200 miles to the south of Jamestown. "No one has yet established a plantation on the northern border of Jamestown," John Carver observed in meeting with a group of Separatist leaders." That area – on the Hudson River near the current location of New York City – became the proposed destination for the Separatist to establish a new settlement.

The Separatist church sent two men, John Carver and Robert Cushman, to England to negotiate with a London stock company about financing a plantation in northern Virginia. While there were significant barriers to overcome during negotiations, in the end, an agreement was reached. Financing was arranged. A ship, the Speedwell, was purchased for the Leiden Separatists to make the voyage to the New World. To the surprise of many, King James gave his approval for the Separatists to create a plantation on the northern border of Virginia. "Better they be across the ocean than close to England!" he exclaimed.

Chapter 21. Beginning of the Journey

The afternoon sun was warm as Elisabeth hurried to meet Rembrandt. They usually met at the bakery, but yesterday Rembrandt suggested they meet at a park along the canal. He was waiting for her and waved when he saw her approaching. As usual, he had fresh bread with him. Elisabeth knew he must have brought it from home because today he had not stopped at the bakery. They broke off chunks from the loaf, savoring its aroma and taste.

"I can't be long," said Elisabeth. "My parents are expecting me at home. We still have packing to complete before we go to the canal boats for tomorrow's journey."

They both looked into the distance, then at one another. "I'll miss you so much, Elisabeth!" said Rembrandt. "I hope your voyage will be safe – and you will enjoy life in the New World."

Then surprising both himself and Elisabeth, he put his arms around her. He had never done that before. Elisabeth could hardly breathe. Should she be afraid of such closeness? What would her father and mother say? Yet the reality of leaving Rembrandt and all that was familiar in Leiden added confusion to the emotions she felt. She was grateful for Rembrandt's friendship. He was kind to her, patient in teaching her to write and read, and so talented in drawing. While the voyage to America seemed at times like an exciting adventure, she felt a surge of sadness about leaving her good friend and all that was familiar. She felt an attachment to Rembrandt – and with his arms now around her, she knew he felt the same.

Too quickly, it seemed, the hug ended. Rembrandt reached inside his coat. He took two parchments from his pocket and handed one to Elisabeth. The one he gave her showed four detailed quill and ink drawings he had created. "Please take my drawings with you, Elisabeth, and when you look at them, you can remember our time together here in Leiden."

Elisabeth looked at the drawings and gasped. Though they were small, she recognized herself in the four sketches – one with a smile she may have had when they watched the cats stalk each other; another with a look of anticipation she might have had when he told her about what he learned at Latin School; another with a sad look she might have shown when she told him of her parents' plan to leave Leiden; and still another with a peaceful look she may have had in telling him about the gratefulness journal she had begun to keep.

"I'll keep your drawing in my journal, Rembrandt. Each time I write in it, I'll think of you." She felt tears come to her eyes.

"I'm keeping one drawing of you," said Rembrandt. "Remember when you were at our home for the Leiden Thanksgiving dinner – and you modeled the red dress and black hat Lysbeth gave you?"

"That was so much fun," said Elisabeth, laughing. "I felt so special in that dress!" He showed her the other parchment. Elisabeth gasped when she saw it. The drawing was clearly one of her wearing the red dress and broad-brimmed hat.

"I'm going to use this drawing to paint a beautiful picture of you someday, Elisabeth."

"Oh, I'd love to see your painting, Rembrandt," said Elisabeth. After a brief pause, she continued, "When it's done, you can send it to me in Virginia." Her statement reminded them both that their time together was at its end.

They looked deeply into one another's eyes, then they both put their arms around each other. Elisabeth felt warm tears flow down her cheeks. "I know we're young," whispered Rembrandt, "but I love you, Elisabeth." Elisabeth's emotions overflowed with a mixture of joy and sadness. Unable to speak, she stood on tiptoes and kissed him. Then she turned and ran toward home. The drawing Rembrandt showed Elisabeth was his first study for his eventual painting, The Girl in a Picture Frame.

That night, July 20th, 1620, Elisabeth and her family – along with 67 other Separatists bound for Virginia – slept for the last time in their homes in Leiden. The next day they left on canal boats for Delfshaven and the ship they would board for the voyage to America, the Speedwell.

Accompanying them as far as Delfshaven were about 40 Separatists from their church congregation. Both groups boarded small boats on the Rapenburg canal which took them south, joining other waterways, and eventually ending in Delfshaven. The 40 who were not going to Virginia made the trip to support those who were making the journey. Pastor John Robinson was among this latter group. "I must stay with the Leiden flock," he told Elder, William Brewster. "You have the wisdom and spiritual maturity to guide these dear people in the New World." However, Pastor Robinson wanted to be on the dock with those leaving for Virginia to share encouragement, hugs, and a final prayer.

The Leiden Separatists stayed the night with friends in Delfshaven. In the morning, a large contingent gathered on the dock to say tearful goodbyes. Pastor Robinson asked everyone to kneel while he prayed for God's blessing and protection – that the lives of each traveler would reflect the fruit of the Spirit - love, joy, peace, patience, kindness, goodness, faithfulness, gentleness, and self-control – and that they would experience God's presence and strength in whatever circumstances they might face. In his prayer, he spoke of the travelers in the context of a biblical passage, referring to them as "strangers and pilgrims" in the new land they were going to.

It would be 200 years before the Separatists were widely referred to as 'Pilgrims'. Daniel Webster used the term during a speech at the Plymouth bicentennial. His comments were based on William Bradford's account of Pastor Robinson's prayer on the Delfshaven dock. Five years after Daniel Webster's speech, Felecia Hemans wrote the classic poem, *The Landing of the Pilgrim Fathers*. Today we attach the name, Pilgrim, to all who made the voyage to Plymouth on the Mayflower.

The time on the Delfshaven dock was a poignant moment in time. Even Dutch residents who had come to watch the Speedwell depart were moved with emotion. Elisabeth could hardly believe the swing in her own feelings: from the sadness of leaving Leiden and Rembrandt to excitement about the momentous adventure ahead. Right now, she just wanted to get on board the ship and get the journey underway. By early afternoon her desire was realized. July 22, 1620, Elisabeth and her parents and 67 other pilgrims boarded the Speedwell with Master Reynolds and crew. Their journey began with the outgoing tide. The first stop would be Southampton where they would meet the Mayflower, the ship that would accompany the Speedwell across the ocean to Virginia.

Two hundred and twenty-three years later, in 1843, artist Robert Weir painted a historical depiction of the Separatists leaving Delfshaven. His painting was entitled, *Embarkation of the Pilgrims*. The original is 12 feet by 18 feet and is hanging in the Rotunda of the US capital. A copy of the painting is on the reverse side of a $10,000 US Federal Reserve note.

Chapter 22. The Speedwell

It took seven days for the Speedwell to complete the passage from Delfshaven to Southampton. The journey was enjoyable for Elisabeth, Desire, and Mary. The ocean swells were gentle; the summer weather warm; the adventure of being on a sailing trip was exciting. Several of the passengers were seasick, but the girls were not. They spent part of their days looking after two infants: Samuel Eaton and Humility Cooper. Samuel's mother was still nursing him, but Humility's mother had died several months previously. Humility's father, Robert, had asked Elisabeth's Aunt Agnes to take Humility on the voyage to Virginia. The girls fed Humility using a spoon and sometimes a cup. Neither baby seemed to be bothered by the motion of the boat.

The girls also helped the Allertons care for their daughter, Mary, aged three. The Allertons' other daughter, five-year-old Remember, did not want to miss anything that her seven-year-old brother Bartholomew found on the ship. He and three other boys of similar age had much to explore.

While the three girls were sitting on the deck one afternoon, Desire commented to Elisabeth and Mary, "Compared to our daily work in Leiden, this trip seems like a holiday."

"How fortunate we are!" Elisabeth responded. "We have no scheduled responsibilities. Here we are with a beautiful view of the ocean, and all we need to stay warm is a sweater."

Onboard the Speedwell was a resident cat, Daisy, who thoroughly enjoyed her responsibility of hunting down mice or rats that found their way on board. However, this voyage presented a new challenge for the cat. John Goodman brought along his two dogs, a mastiff named Sadie, and a springer spaniel, Missy. The dogs, of course, felt it was their duty to try to apprehend Daisy. "I wonder if the dogs have thought about what would happen if they actually caught up to Daisy?" Elisabeth asked her friends. "I saw one of our cats at the bakery use her claws to send a poor dog scampering."

Daisy seemed to know all the locations she could fit where the dogs could not, and it seemed like Daisy's safe spots were always just around a corner. The poor dogs skidded around the corners in hot pursuit, but the decks had little traction, and the dogs' back legs usually spun out and went from underneath them. The frequent chases provided good belly laughs for the passengers.

Some leaks appeared in the Speedwell hull during the trip to Southampton, but Master Reynolds did not seem visibly concerned. "We will correct that problem as soon as we reach Southampton," he assured the passengers. Privately, he was not so sure, or as some said later, perhaps he was quite satisfied that the leaks occurred as planned. The unexpected seepage could have been due to stress on the hull from a new, more substantial mast that had been installed – or leaks could have been orchestrated so that the ship would be found unseaworthy for an ocean crossing.

Chapter 23. Southampton

On the evening of July 29th, 1620, the Speedwell sailed into Southampton harbor with the incoming tide. The sun had not yet set, and many of the passengers were on the deck to view the approach, even though they had to look out for quickly moving sailors and lines that sometimes lashed unexpectedly.

The crew of the Speedwell dropped anchor near the Mayflower, the ship they were to sail with across the Atlantic. The Mayflower had arrived in Southampton a few days earlier, having sailed from the Thames near London. The Speedwell passengers were impressed with the size of Mayflower. She was at least twice the length of the Speedwell and had an additional third mast. The Mayflower was in fact, 112 feet long from the back rail to the front of the bowsprit, and about 25 feet wide.

Passengers and cargo were already aboard the Mayflower. The ship and her Master, Christopher Jones, were ready to leave Southampton; however, the leak in the Speedwell required immediate attention. Master Reynolds guided the Speedwell to a dock, and the ship's carpenter and crew worked on repairs for several days.

In the meantime, the Robert Cushman family, who had been on the Mayflower, came over to the Speedwell to visit with Leiden friends. The Cushmans had lived in Holland for several years and formed strong friendships. Robert had been in England for the past two years, working with John Carver to negotiate with the Virginia Company for a plantation patent in northern Virginia and arrange for financing of the voyage.

The Cushmans brought news with them that a sizable contingent of passengers on the Mayflower were not Separatists. "Costs for the voyage to Virginia have continued to mount," he reported. "Our investors refused to add additional funding. They said that the only way to raise the extra capital was to find paying passengers. We resisted and protested, but in the end, the choice was between canceling the voyage and losing our investment – or accepting the paying passengers.

While the Separatists were not happy about the inclusion of passengers who were not of their religious persuasion, funds were not available to demand an alternative. They had sold their homes and all but essential possessions to invest in the voyage. Turning back to England or Leiden was not a practical option. As the Separatists forged forward, they captured the differences between themselves and other passengers by referring to others as 'Strangers' and to their own group as 'Saints.' As it turned out, slightly more than half the passengers who made the trip to the New World were Strangers.

It was August 5th before both ships were ready to leave Southampton harbor.

Chapter 24. Attempts to Sail from England

The passengers and crews of both vessels were relieved to finally be underway. For Elisabeth and friends, the voyage along the south coast of England was an extension of the enjoyable Speedwell voyage from Holland. The ocean swell was light, and the summer winds, though fresh, did not yet have the chill of fall.

But all was not well with the Speedwell. The repairs undertaken in Southampton harbor had not stopped leaks in the hull. After seven days of westward sailing, both ships pulled into Dartmouth. It was August 11th. This time, it took the better part of nine days for additional repairs to be completed on the Speedwell's hull.

On August 20th, Master Reynolds declared the Speedwell ready to sail. The following day both ships again headed out for their trans-ocean voyage. On day seven, they sailed past Land's End, the south-west tip of England, and out into the North Atlantic.

By this time, the holiday nature of the voyage had worn off for virtually all passengers on both ships. They had been on board for over a month, and many continued to suffer from seasickness; however, the problems they experienced were just the beginning of what would be an unimaginably difficult crossing. About 300 miles past Land's End, Master Reynolds concluded his ship would not survive an ocean crossing. Leaks in the hull were once again too severe to continue. He signaled Master Jones of the Mayflower, and both ships turned back toward England.

Both ships docked in Plymouth. If the voyage to northern Virginia was to continue, it was clear that the Speedwell would need to be left behind with the Mayflower continuing on her own. Doing so meant some passengers could not make the trip. There simply was not enough room on the Mayflower to accommodate all passengers from both ships. For some, it was a relief to disembark and stay in England. The stress of a leaky boat, seasickness, and crowded, close conditions had already been too much. Of the 132 passengers who had been on the two ships, only 102 would continue.

Chapter 25. Hazelnuts

During the few days it took to move cargo from the Speedwell to the Mayflower, Elisabeth, Desire, and Mary took advantage of the time to go for long walks near Plymouth. "We won't have opportunity to walk in the countryside until we get to Virginia," Elisabeth reminded Desire and Mary. "Let's walk while we can."

The opportunity for fresh air and freedom to move about was a welcome change for the girls. The Speedwell had little room to move about, and even though the Mayflower was a larger ship, they knew conditions would be cramped.

On an outing during their second day, the girls met a young couple who, with their two children, were about to go into a grove of hazelnut trees to gather nuts. The couple introduced themselves as Donald and Susan, and their children as Adam and Dinah.

"Where are you from?" Susan asked the girls. The girls gave a brief explanation of their trip from Holland, and the upcoming voyage to Virginia. The couple were taken with the sense of adventure and courage that the journey represented.

"What a daring journey you're on!" exclaimed Donald. "How long will it take to get to Virginia?"

"We think it will be about a month to sail there," replied Elisabeth.

The young couple marveled at the thought of such a voyage. "That's such a long time to be on a ship!" said Susan. "What do you eat when you're on a ship for so long?"

"The food is a bit boring," responded Mary. "There's only so much you can do with salted pork and hardtack."

Susan thought for a moment, then said, "You know, last winter some friends shared their store of hazelnuts with us, and we really loved them as a snack. The children enjoyed them too, so we decided to gather our own store of nuts this year."

She looked for a moment at Donald and then said to the girls, "We could share some hazelnuts with you. You won't have time to dry the nuts we gather today before you go, but you could have some of our supply. We gathered our first batch a couple weeks ago, so they'll be dried enough to eat by now. You could help us gather more hazelnuts today. We'll take them home to dry, and you can have some of the nuts we've already dried to take with you on your ship."

The girls looked at one another, and almost simultaneously said, "Great idea!"

Susan and Don already had their own baskets for gathering nuts, and the girls each used their long skirts to hold the nuts they gathered. Many hazelnuts were already on the ground, and Donald helped create a greater supply by shaking tree branches. Within a short time, the group had as much as they could carry, and returned to the young couples' abode.

"What a lovely home you have here," said Elisabeth. It was a three-room structure, similar to what Elisabeth remembered in Henlow: most space taken up by the cooking and living area, a smaller bedroom, and a washroom. It didn't take long for Susan to give the girls a tour.

Donald searched through some of the couple's belongings and found two stones. They were slightly larger than the girls' fists. Both stones had a flat side, but one had a hollow in the flat surface. He sat down at the table and said, "Let me demonstrate how I crack the nuts. I usually place the rock with the hollow on a table like this," he showed them. "Put a hazelnut in the hollow of this stone, then hit it with this flatter rock like this." He hit the rocks sharply together. When he took the rocks apart, the girls saw how the shell had cracked, leaving the meat of the nut intact.

"Sometimes a nut doesn't crack quite enough, and you need to hit it more than once, or if the nuts are too big, the meat inside the shell gets squashed – but most of the time it works well." He said. "Here, each of you try shelling one."

The girls each took a turn cracking a nut or two, and after observing their success, Donald pronounced them proficient. Susan gave the girls two baskets filled with dried nuts. "I know we'll enjoy these," said Desire. "We've eaten nothing but salted pork, salted fish, pickles, and hardtack on the Speedwell for almost a month, and our food on the Mayflower probably will be the same. The hazelnuts will be a welcome break!"

After warm hugs with the family, the girls began their walk back to the Plymouth docks and the Mayflower. On the way, they each remarked about how much they enjoyed the visit to Susan's and Donald's home. "I wonder what our homes in Virginia will be like?" Mary asked the others. The girls were lost in thought for a time until Elisabeth responded with another thought-provoking question, "I wonder if we will find husbands and have our own families there?" They continued in silence until they reached the Mayflower.

Chapter 26. Finally - The Voyage Begins

On September 6, 1620 - based on the Julian calendar in use in England at that time - the crew of the Mayflower took up the lines at the dock in Plymouth. According to the Gregorian calendar, later adopted in England and the calendar we currently use, the date was September 16th. The transfer off the ship of passengers who decided to stay in England and the transfer of passengers and cargo from the Speedwell to the Mayflower was completed. The winds and tide were favorable for moving the ship out to sea. The journey across the Atlantic was underway – this time, everyone hoped, until the crossing was completed. The ship had a crew of 30 sailors and 102 passengers. Fewer than half the passengers were Saints; the larger group were Strangers – people who did not necessarily share the religious beliefs of the Separatists.

Even though the Mayflower was a larger ship than the Speedwell, the conditions on board were terribly crowded. All passengers were housed on the gun deck, located immediately below the main deck. While the main deck provided shelter from sun and rain to passengers on the gun deck, the gun deck was something like a dark crawl-space with a five-and-a-half-foot high ceiling. Even though most of the passengers were not that tall, the space made them all feel like they needed to walk with their heads lowered.

The total area for the gun deck was 80 feet long and 25 feet wide. One hundred two people, two dogs, four pigs, four sheep, and a dozen chickens vied for space. In addition, the gun deck held parts for a shallop, a small sailing vessel that would be used in shallow waters when the Mayflower reached the shores of Virginia. The pieces would be re-assembled when they reached their destination. Another smaller vessel, a longboat, was also housed on the gun deck.

Privacy was almost non-existent, apart from cloth curtains and a few wood partitions passengers erected. Families brought along chamber pots for relieving themselves. All the passengers were accustomed to using chamber pots on land, but the ship provided unique challenges in using them. Part of the problem was simply in finding privacy. In addition, it was difficult using the chamber pots as the ship rolled from side to side. Whether individuals were relieving themselves or vomiting from seasickness, the chamber pots were sometimes missed. And then, of course, there was the task of getting the chamber pots emptied overboard.

Chapter 27. Social Groupings on Board

The demographic make-up of the passengers on the Mayflower was a cross-section of humanity. There were two infants on board, along with 2-year old Damaris Hopkins.

Fourteen children were in the 3 – 12 age range, including six boys who were 5 -7 years old. The younger children stayed mostly with their parents, but the six boys explored the ship together as much as parents and sailors would allow.

Richard Tinker, who was ten and William Latham, 11, hung out with Giles Hopkins, 12, and John Hooke, who was 13.

Six teenaged girls had no problem keeping occupied in assisting harried mothers to care for and watch over younger children. Elisabeth Tilley, Desire Minter, and Mary Chilton had already formed a bond in Leiden. They welcomed Constance Hopkins into their friendship, and all four were grateful that two 19-year-olds, Priscilla Mullins and Dorothy Jones, were willing to spend much of their time with them. Priscilla was on board with her parents and young brother, Joseph. Dorothy worked with the Carver family.

One cause that drew the six girls together was the More children. They seemed so sad! Their father had taken custody of them as an outcome of a bitter divorce settlement. Believing the children were not really his, and to spite his ex-wife, he paid Mayflower investors to have them placed with families who were sailing on the Mayflower: Ellen, 8, with the Winslows, her brother Jasper, 7, with the Carvers, and Richard, 6, and Mary, 4, with the Brewsters. The children missed their mother terribly. Elisabeth and her friends did their best to support the children by telling them stories, holding the younger ones on their laps, or making sure they received their daily allotment of food and beer.

Elisabeth made good friends with John Goodman's smaller dog, a spaniel named Missy. Missy liked to be close to people, and she seemed to sense when someone was apprehensive. When the More children sat with Elisabeth, Missy moved close to them, pressing her body gently against theirs. Elisabeth wondered if Missy recognized the children's sadness and that pressing close to them was Missy's way of providing consolation. Whether or not Missy's closeness was intentional, Elisabeth could tell it brought comfort to the children.

There were 17 teenage boys on board, some with their parents, while others were servants to families. The boys did not form strong relationships with one another; however, they all seemed to disdain two of their group, the rambunctious Billington boys.

There were 18 adult women on board. All were married, and three were pregnant: Elizabeth Hopkins, Susanna White, and Mary Allerton. All three women were later to give birth on board the Mayflower.

Twenty-three married men were on the voyage. Five had left wives in Leiden with a plan to bring them to Virginia once the colony was adequately developed. Twenty-one single men over the age of 21 brought the adult male total to 44.

The initial days and weeks of the voyage were tolerable for some passengers. Others who suffered from seasickness felt worse than miserable. On a tour of the gun deck, one of the sailors remarked, "The first stage of seasickness is when you feel you might die; the second stage is when you're afraid you won't." Sometimes those who were sick were close enough to a chamber pot to use it, and sometimes they just weren't. The misses began to add to growing uncleanliness and a terrible stench on the gun deck.

Despite the unsanitary conditions, Elisabeth and the other teen girls did their best to encourage one another, and at times, look on the lighter side of life. In one of their conversations, Priscilla Mullins said to the others, "Do you know how many boys and men on this ship have the first name of John?" The girls laughed. Desire Minter said, "There must be at least a dozen Johns."

"You're close," said Priscilla. "I counted 14! If someone shouted, 'John! Come here!' we could get trampled!"

They all had a good laugh at Priscilla's observation. "Yes," added Elisabeth, "it's much easier to know who's who when people name their children like the Brewster's did. How many boys do you know with the names of Love and Wrestling? What do you say we make up some nicknames for our Johns?"

The girls had many good laughs together, proposing nicknames for all the different Johns on board. Unfortunately, only one suggestion found its way beyond the group. One of the girls suggested the nickname, Sam, for John Howland.

"Why Sam?" someone asked.

"Because I think he's built like Samson," came the reply – and a chorus of laughter from the others.

Chapter 28. The Mean-Spirited Sailor

One of the sailors who frequently came to the gun deck went out of his way to be verbally abusive to the passengers. "What a stinkin' lot you are!" he shouted at them. "You're pukin' all over one another. I can't believe how bad you smell! I hope I get to slide a bunch of you overboard before we get to Virginia! That way we'll have less to unload when we get there."

The sailor's verbal assaults came daily. He took every opportunity to insult and curse the passengers. Elder William Brewster exhorted others to pay no attention to the sailor, and even to pray for him. "God will deal with him in His own way," he said repeatedly. But it was impossible to ignore the sailor's rude and crude attacks.

On one occasion when the sailor came to the passenger deck, he noticed Elisabeth, Desire, and Mary cracking hazelnuts. "What have you got there, girls?" he asked. "Have you been hiding treats from me? I'll have some of those if you don't mind," he announced as he grabbed a handful of nuts from their basket. "If I like these, I'll be back for more. Stupid girls," he mocked.

There was nothing the girls or others could do to stop the sailor. He laughed as he climbed the rope ladder to the upper deck. "What stinking, miserable wretches you are," he shouted. "Soon, I'll get to throw some of you overboard!"

That evening in a small cabin he shared with other sailors near the back of the upper deck, the sailor cracked a handful of hazelnuts he had taken from the girls. "Look at what those young girls gave to me," he laughed, showing them to another sailor. "Can't wait to taste them."

He tried one of the shelled nuts, enjoying the flavor and texture. He felt an itching in his mouth and a tingling in his lips, but thinking nothing of it, threw several more nuts into his mouth. Within minutes, his lips began to swell, and his throat tightened so that breathing became labored. Realizing something was wrong, his cabin-mate took the sailor in search of the ship's doctor, Giles Heale. Dr. Heale recognized the seriousness of the sailor's condition but had no idea of how to treat him. The sailor's breathing became increasingly labored, and he began to complain of pain in his abdomen.

Dr. Heale sent the sailor's friend to the gun deck to call Samuel Fuller, who Dr. Heale knew to be an experienced medical practitioner. Dr. Fuller came, bringing with him Elder Brewster. By now the sailor was barely able to speak. As the doctors consulted with one another, Elder Brewster held the man's hand and prayed for him. "Thank you, Father, that you love this man. Help him to experience your love and forgiveness." Elder Brewster could see that the sailor's condition was desperate. Dr. Fuller grasped the sailor's other hand. Both men saw fear and gratefulness in the sailor's eyes. Within 10 minutes the sailor could draw no more life-giving air. His body convulsed and then was still.

Other crew members wrapped the body of the sailor in cloth and tied rocks to his ankles. They carried him to the deck rail. Elder Brewster prayed as they committed the sailor to the sea. The sailor who mocked the passengers so mercilessly became the first on the voyage to be buried overboard.

A new sense of respect for the Saints came upon the crew and officers. Even Master Jones showed new respect. The sailor had gone out of his way to be meanspirited to the passengers. Was his death due to his malicious treatment of the Saints? Could the crew have just witnessed God's judgment? While the voyage did not get any easier for anyone on board, the Master of the ship and his crew went out of their way to be as respectful as possible to the passengers.

Chapter 29. Overboard

A month into the voyage, the weather changed. The strong but steady head winds and large but smooth ocean swells turned to high, gusty winds and enormous, breaking waves - creating stormy conditions that Master Jones had seldom seen. The North Atlantic could have a fury that fully challenged both ships and mariners, and this part of the voyage taxed both. The wind and waves were so ferocious that at times, Master Jones commanded all sails to be furled. The Mayflower was at the mercy of the elements. The good news was that in such situations, the ship was stable, even as it rolled with the enormous waves.

Meanwhile, conditions on the gun deck continued to deteriorate. The smell from spilled chamber pots and vomit grew increasingly dreadful. Passenger John Howland had had quite enough. Even though a storm waged, he simply needed fresh air and perhaps a glimpse of the horizon. He climbed the rope ladder to the main deck. The sweet smell of fresh sea air was a welcome relief. As he looked across the deck at the ocean, the size of the swells amazed him.   Waves towered above the Mayflower, and John wondered how the ship managed to climb such massive walls of water. He held tightly to whatever was at hand, making his way towards the middle of the deck.

John glanced behind him to see the pilot in the steerage room, waving wildly. "He probably thinks this isn't very safe for me," was the thought that went through John's mind. "I better go back to the gun deck."

As John let his grip go to turn around, an extraordinarily large wave crashed over the deck. Before he knew it, John was engulfed in the water and swept overboard. 'Terrifying' only begins to describe his experience. John's later recollection of his thoughts going overboard was, "No!! God help me! I'll be a disappointment to Mr. Carver!" Despite being underwater, he recalled his eyes being wide open. He was aware of the darkness of the water and the lightness of the bubbles. The screaming of the wind stopped.

John felt a sickening helplessness. It was not possible to fight the power and immensity of the ocean. Though young, strong, and well built, there was nothing he could do but hold his breath until he could hold it no longer.

At first, he saw it, then he felt it against his leg. A line was in the water. John lunged his left arm outward and felt the coarse, hardness of hemp rope in his hand. He grabbed ahold with his left hand and pulled the line toward himself until he could grasp it with his right hand as well. Then the line went slack, and he felt himself start to sink. His boots and wool clothing were heavy, dragging him down. Two thoughts simultaneously flashed into John's thoughts: "I'm still alive!" and "How will I ever get to the surface?"

As a wave moved the ship away from John's location, the line became taut. The force dragged him rapidly through the water and toward the surface. His hands, then his head broke the surface. He gasped for air and immediately saw that the line he held onto was attached to the ship. A rope that should have been neatly coiled on deck had also washed overboard and was dragging in the water. John recalled feeling no sense of chill from the water. He only felt the urgency to hold the line connecting him to the ship. His grip was vice-like. Letting go meant certain death. He would hold on until he could hold on no longer.

Then the ship was pushed back toward him, causing the line to slacken. Without the pull of the line, John again began to sink. He had no idea how deep he went but felt the increasing water pressure in his ears. Then the line abruptly tightened as the ship lurched away, and once again, John was dragged upward toward the surface.

Fortunately for John, the pilot and two sailors with him in the steerage room saw that he was swept overboard. "He's gone!" the pilot shouted. The two sailors continued to stare out at where John had stood on the deck, and then in the direction he was washed overboard. As they watched, both men noticed a line that had become taut. They looked at one another and then at the pilot, and then all three said almost in unison, "No! It's not possible!" As their eyes followed the taut line they soon saw John's arms and head surface briefly. "He can't hold on long out there," the pilot shouted, "See if you can get him in."

With a line tied to their waist and the other end tied to the ship, the two sailors ventured out on deck. They both looked in the direction of the taut line, and saw John surface once again. "He's still there!" one shouted into the wind.

Without further conversation, the sailors worked their way to where the trailing line was connected to the ship. They began the task of hauling the line back to the ship, feeling the resistance of the man at the end as he was dragged through the water. While the sailors knew they had to try to save the man who had gone overboard, they both said afterward that they thought it was unlikely anyone could hold on that long in the cold water.

It was a slow process, but the sailors hauled John close to the ship. A wave slammed his body against the hull. As the vessel continued to roll, his body and the ocean level came close to the deck rail. When the ship leaned the other way, he was at least ten feet below the rail. One of the sailors detached a nearby gaff hook. When the ship next rolled so that John was within reach, the sailor hooked the back of John's pants. Together the two sailors hauled on the gaff-hook, and like a large fish, flopped John onto the deck. He still held the line tightly. The sailors dragged him away from the rail and over to the door of the forecastle, which served as the ship's galley. Before getting him inside, it took the efforts of both sailors to pry John's fingers from the rope. Realizing that John had just been hauled out of the ocean, the cook tolerated his presence on the floor of the forecastle.

One of the sailors went to the gun deck to ask the passengers for a blanket for John. Meanwhile, John lay exhausted. Fortunately, he had not swallowed much seawater, so he was not sick to his stomach. Had he been, the cook would likely have pushed him out of the forecastle right away. Instead, the cook allowed John to lay on the floor near the stove to warm his exhausted body. Finally, John felt enough strength to remove his soaking boots and clothes and wrap himself in the blanket.

The cook poured some boiling water into a mug and said to John, "You are one lucky bloke! You'll be the only passenger on this ship to get a cup of hot tea from me."

Late in the day, John felt strong enough and warm enough to thank the cook, take his leave from the forecastle, and make his way to the gun deck.

The passengers had heard a commotion on deck when John went overboard. John Carver had known his trusted servant – and friend - John Howland had gone up on deck. Mr. Carver had climbed the rope ladder far enough to hear sailors shouting back and forth about what had happened. He shared with Elder Brewster, Samuel Fuller, and others about the misfortune so they could pray for John. Desire Minter and Dorothy Jones, both part of the extended Carver family, heard about the tragedy and told Elisabeth, Mary, Constance, and Priscilla. All the girls assumed the worst – that there would be no chance of saving John. Why could such a nice person be so horribly lost? Several passengers took turns on the rope ladder to try to glimpse what was transpiring on deck but could not see the sailors who were engaged in the unlikely task of rescuing John while a storm raged about the ship.

John Howland's descent down the rope ladder was an emotional high and a breathtaking bright spot in the middle of an increasingly bleak voyage. One hundred one passengers cheered and clapped as John descended to the gun deck – and a number cried with joy. Surely it was God's intervention! What other explanation could there be for someone - washed overboard and presumed drowned - to be miraculously brought back on the ship?

Elder Brewster led the group in a thanksgiving prayer. He then said, "John, my son, God has a special purpose for you. He has brought you back from the depths of the sea for a reason. Praise be to God!" Among the many who hugged John and expressed gratefulness that he was safe was Elisabeth Tilley. "I'm so glad you're safe, John, and that God yet has a purpose for you," she said, looking directly into his eyes. While others expressed similar sentiments, neither Elisabeth nor John – nor anyone else on the Mayflower - imagined the beautiful relationship that would grow between Elisabeth and John over the next 53 years.

Chapter 30. Rogue Wave

Storms were a constant for the remainder of the voyage. The degree of severity was the only variable. The Mayflower was inching toward America, averaging barely two miles per hour.

It had been over 40 days since the Mayflower had left Plymouth, and another 40 days since passengers had boarded the Mayflower at Blackwell, or the Speedwell at Delfshaven. Many of the passengers had lost a sense of time, and their general well-being was deteriorating. The constant diet of salt pork, fish, and hardtack kept their stomachs partially full but did not provide the nourishment needed to sustain their bodies. The drink for all passengers and crew was beer. It was the only beverage that would not spoil in barrels during of an extended voyage. Fresh, drinkable water was rare in England and certainly did not last long on board a ship. Infants, children, and adults had a daily quota of almost a gallon of beer.

On day 42, a near disaster struck the Mayflower. A rogue wave hit the ship so hard that the passengers on the gun deck thought the boat would break in two. The thunder of the wave smashing against the hull and on the deck was deafening; passengers and crew heard a loud crack, and the ship shuddered. A beam that spanned the middle of the gun deck fractured. Water cascaded onto the gun deck through every possible gap. Many of the passengers screamed. Some – and soon all the passengers - noticed the broken beam. They could see movement of the two separate parts. Surely the ship was about to break apart, and all would be cast into the ocean.

John Carver hurried up the rope ladder to alert the crew. Master Jones, mate Robert Coppin, and ship's carpenter John Alden were already making their way cautiously along the upper deck, checking stays on the masts. Each crew member had a line tied about their waist, the other end secured to the ship. The Master was concerned something might have broken but was not sure what it was. Pilot John Clarke remained at the helm in the steerage room.

John Alden was the first crewman to see Carver waving to get their attention. He made his way to the opening, and Carver told him about the beam. Alden's foot barely touched the floor of the gun deck when he saw the cracked beam. He hurried back up the ladder and waved to the Master and mate. They hastened to follow John down to the gun deck. The three men knew immediately that the ship was in grave danger. John Alden stated the situation to the others almost clinically. "We need to stabilize the beam right away. If another wave breaks on the deck, support for the main deck and the hull will not be sufficient. The ship is almost certain to break in two."

A number of the passengers congregated near the ship's officers and carpenter. Among those who overheard the hushed but intense conversation was Francis Eaton. He was a carpenter and house builder and was the passenger responsible for insisting that a heavy-duty screw jack be taken along for the voyage to help in house construction at the new colony. "There is a large screw-jack in the hold below us," Francis told John Alden. "We could use it to support the beam and keep it from collapsing."

"Absolutely that would work!" said John. "Let's get it up here."

Accessing the jack from the hold below the gun deck, meant they had to remove a hatch. It required passengers to shift or relocate on an already crowded deck. John and Francis removed the hatch and carried an oil lamp with them to look for the jack. As might be expected, the jack was not easy to access. The two men called for help. Four of the most robust passengers came to assist: John Howland, Isaac Allerton, John Goodman, and Edward Doty came forward and descended into the hold. As Goodman disappeared into the hold, his dogs, Sadie and Missy, thought they should be going as well, and barked excitedly until they heard John's sharp command for them to stop. Both dogs stood by the open hatch with tails wagging and tongues hanging out, waiting for John to reappear.

The men managed to lift the jack out of the hold and onto the gun deck, then slide it along the deck and below the cracked beam. With the two men holding a stout timber steady on the top of the jack and two others holding a similar support in place under the base of the jack, John Alden turned the screw until the top timber made contact with the beam, then lifted it slightly so that the beam assumed an almost natural position.

"Well done, men!" said Master Jones. The jack remained in place, supporting the beam until John Alden made a more permanent restoration while the ship anchored near Plymouth.

As Alden turned from patching the beam to ascend the rope ladder, he noticed a group of relieved passengers watching him. One face stood out: that of a girl about his age. Their eyes locked for an instant. John started up the ladder, then looked around once more to find the girl, but she was gone. "I hope no more beams break down here," he thought to himself. "But I sure will come down to recheck this one – and find out who that girl is." The girl would turn out to be Priscilla Mullins, and while there were many hurdles to overcome, in 18 months, John and Priscilla would marry in Plymouth.

Chapter 31. A New Passenger

In the awful conditions on the gun deck, somewhere in the middle of the North Atlantic, Elizabeth Hopkins went into labor. Six hours later she gave birth to a son. She and husband Stephen named him Oceanus. Several women held blankets to help with privacy during the birthing process. Given the difficulty of the voyage and the unsanitary conditions, many wondered privately whether there would be much future for the newborn.

The child's father, Stephen Hopkins, was a true survivor. He was the only passenger on board who had previously crossed the ocean. In 1609, eleven years earlier, he had sailed to Jamestown, Virginia, but before arriving, was shipwrecked in Bermuda. He and the other passengers and crew either repaired their ship or managed to build another vessel. Eventually, they made it to Jamestown. A few years later, Stephen returned to England, but when he did, he discovered that his first wife had died. In 1616, he had met and married Elizabeth.

Stephen was aboard the Mayflower because the business partners who helped fund the voyage felt his expertise was needed to support the new colony. They hoped the survival skills he gained in Bermuda and his experience with Native Americans in Jamestown would contribute to the success of a new plantation.

Chapter 32. Land Sighted

On November 6th, day 63 of the voyage, Dr. Fuller's servant William Butten, died. His body was wrapped in cloth and committed to the sea.

Dr. Fuller observed similar conditions in many of the passengers as he saw in young William. He spoke privately with John Carver and William Brewster, "We need to get our people off the ship and into more sanitary conditions as soon as possible," he told them. "And it may be that our limited diet is a factor," he added. A keen observer, Dr. Fuller noticed the relatively good health of the teenaged girls. He wondered if it could possibly have any connection to the hazelnuts they ate. Apart from the nuts, everyone had the same diet.

Three days later on November 9th, the spirits of passengers were lifted. A sailor sighted land. Excitement quickly spread throughout the ship. Master Jones and his pilot, John Clarke, examined charts and calculated the ship's location as accurately as possible. "We are a few degrees north of the Hudson River," Master Jones announced. "The land ahead is New England."

Master Jones consulted briefly with Elder Brewster and John Carver about their location and agreed to turn the ship south to the Hudson River area of Virginia. However, unknown to Master Jones and the pilot, the waters immediately to the east of Cape Cod were among the most dangerous on the east coast of America. The ship nearly ran aground on shoals. Fortunately, on the northern edge of the shoals, the wind shifted to the southwest, pushing the Mayflower away from imminent danger. The sailors could hardly believe their good fortune in avoiding what looked like a catastrophe. The near-disaster was not lost on Elder Brewster or John Carver, who were with Master Jones at the time. Brewster observed, "Once again, God answered our prayers. He controls even the winds!"

Beyond the immediate danger to the ship from shoals along the eastern coast of Cape Cod, Master Jones was well aware of the growing health crisis among the passengers, and even his crew. In addition, provisions were getting low, and he still had a return voyage to England ahead of him. Conditions all pointed to having tempted fate far enough. His ship would no longer try to reach the Hudson River area of Virginia. He turned to William Brewster and John Carver and said, "We cannot continue further south. We've come perilously close to running aground on shoals we did not know about. Beyond the safety of the ship, many passengers and some of my crew are in poor health. We must find a location for a settlement nearby."

Brewster and Carver understood the gravity of the situation and did not try to change Master Jones' mind. He gave orders to direct the ship into Cape Cod Bay. They would search there for a suitable location for a settlement.

News of the change in plans created a range of reactions in passengers. Some thought that since they were not landing in northern Virginia, they were no longer held to the terms of the contract they had signed with the Virginia Company. "We can make up our own rules now," John Billington said to anyone who would listen. "If we're not going to Virginia, we cannot be bound by the contract we signed." Several passengers agreed with him. Others recognized the need for synergy. Dr. Fuller was one of them. "If we do not work together, survival of any of us will be unlikely," he countered.

Elder Brewster had, on several sleepless nights, considered the possibility of the Mayflower arriving at a destination other than northern Virginia. What would they do? How would they organize themselves? The seeds of how they might agree to live together had begun to form in his mind. Now that a settlement outside of Virginia became a necessity for survival, Brewster brought those thoughts forward, and on November 10th , penned what is now known as the Mayflower Compact. It briefly and succinctly set forth an agreement to live as an orderly group, to enact laws as needed for the general good of the colony, and agreement to obey such laws.

Elder Brewster shared the written document with John Carver and Master Jones. "I need you both to read this document and tell me what you think," he said. The two read it while Brewster waited.

"It has the essential principles needed for a civil settlement," Carver said. "I agree," added Master Jones. "I will order all adult male passengers to gather here in my quarters in the morning. Mr. Brewster, you read the document and provide any explanation they ask for. I will tell them they must sign it before any of them step ashore."

The next morning, November 11th, just before entering Provincetown Harbor inside the northwest corner of Cape Cod, Master Jones commanded that all adult male passengers 21 years of age and older assemble at his quarters near the rear of the ship. Forty-one men listened attentively as Brewster read the document.

Talk quickly turned to who should lead the group. Stephen Hopkins suggested John Carver. "I sat in on some of the negotiations in London," Stephen said. "John argued persuasively and passionately on behalf of all who would embark on this voyage, but he also knew when to compromise."

"We held John Carver in high esteem in Leiden," added John Tilley. "We know him to be a man of wisdom and patience."

"I agree with what these two men have said," added John Howland. "I work daily with Mr. Carver and have seen his expertise first-hand. His people skills and business acumen never cease to amaze me."

No other names were put forward. "Are you willing to lead this group?" asked Master Jones. "I am," responded Carver.

"Raise your hand if you are willing to have John Carver as Governor of your new settlement," Master Jones said to the assembled group. Agreement was unanimous.

"Now, each of you affix your signatures here," Master Jones said, pointing to the document. The custom of the day was that women did not sign such papers, nor did anyone under the age of 21; however, when the men left Master Jones' quarters and returned to the gun deck, the new Governor went out of his way to explain the Mayflower Compact to all passengers so that everyone had a good understanding of what it meant. In the end, they all felt they were a part of the agreement.

Before noon on November 11th, 1620, the Mayflower dropped anchor in what is now known as Provincetown Harbor.

Chapter 33. Provincetown Harbor

The first full day in Provincetown Harbor was a Sunday. Passengers stayed on board for worship. On Monday, November 13th, they could hardly wait to get off the ship. Men took the disassembled parts of the shallop ashore to reconstruct it.

Elisabeth, her five teen friends, and four adult women took the occasion to go ashore for a hike. Other women on board declined the opportunity to go. They were either sick or had no energy. Not far inland, the women found fresh water.

Mary Chilton was the first to try a sip. "The water is sweet!" she exclaimed. "Taste it!" The others cupped their hands and tasted the water.

"You're right, Mary," said Priscilla Mullins. It's better than any water I ever tasted in England!" "And better than any we had in Holland," added Elisabeth.

"You know what," said Desire, "we can wash our clothes here!"

"What a great idea!" responded Dorothy. "Our clothing and bedding are disgustingly dirty. They look awful, and I can hardly stand the smell! Let's get back to the ship, and bring our laundry here." The ten women returned to the Mayflower, gathered what they could carry and came back to the pool. It was the first day of a tradition for Elisabeth and others in their new setting: wash Monday.

The Mayflower anchored in Provincetown Harbor for a month. During this time, groups of men went on exploratory expeditions on land to look for a suitable place to establish a settlement, and search for native inhabitants. Even Master Jones and a group of sailors accompanied the men on one excursion. Jones was anxious for the group to find a settlement location so he could get the people and their belongings off his ship and sail back to England. When the shallop was finally assembled and seaworthy, the men used it to explore further afield around Cape Cod Bay.

On one of the expeditions, the men came across a rise in the sand they could see was smoothly packed. "What do you think is under there?" one of the group asked, pointing to the mound. "There's one way to find out," was the response. Digging into the sand, the men discovered a basket containing dried corn, still on the cob. "Here's food for a few weeks!" was the first reaction.

However, one member of the expedition responded, "We can't take this corn. It's been carefully buried. It must belong to people who live near here."

One of the sailors on the expedition observed, "It may belong to someone else, but your food supply is already low. It will be a few months before you can grow your own. Take what you've found. When you grow your food next summer, you can repay whoever buried their corn here."

It didn't take further persuasion. Each man knew their growing desperation. This food cache might well mean the difference between survival and starvation. They carried it with them back to the Mayflower.

There was a very real sense that the men were indeed fortunate to have a ship to come back to. While they were away, 14-year old Francis Billington found his father's musket. "Hey John," he said to his older brother. "Look at this! I found dad's rifle. I bet I could shoot something!"

"You have no idea how to fire a rifle, you idiot," John's brother told him. "Put it down before you hurt yourself."

Francis didn't put the gun down. He played with it until he accidentally fired it – or maybe he knew what he was doing and had to show his older brother he really could fire the weapon. Whatever the motivation, Francis was beside an open door leading to the gun room. Sparks from the firing sprayed into the gun room close to an open barrel of gunpowder. Had the barrel ignited, other barrels of gunpowder would have blown up, and the ship itself would have been lost. Two of the men who had remained on board hurried over to take the gun away from Frances.

On November 28th, while the Mayflower was in Provincetown Harbor, Susanna White went into labor and gave birth to a son. "If this little one is nothing else," she said, "he's a traveler. I'm going to name him Peregrine." Despite the difficult conditions, mother and son were unexpectedly strong and healthy. Other passengers were not.

While William Bradford and a group of other men were out searching for a settlement site, William's wife, Dorothy, ascended to the main deck of the Mayflower even though it was bitterly cold. "The air is so foul down here," she told Mrs. Carver, "I need to get up for a breath of fresh air."

"Do be careful, Dear," responded Mrs. Carver. "It's even colder on deck than it is down here."

Dorothy noticed it was cold enough on the main deck for ice to form in patches. She wondered how her poor husband and those exploring with him could survive the wind and snow. She searched the distance for any sign of their return. Wondering if she saw something, she kept her eye on the horizon and stepped closer to the ship's rail. With her focus on seeing her husband and his party in the distance, she did not notice she was standing on a patch of ice. Leaning forward to get a better look, she slipped and fell overboard. The fall to the water was not far, but her wool clothing immediately carried her under the surface. Her body was never recovered.

Exploration of Cape Cod Bay – south from Provincetown Harbor, around the Bay and back northward - convinced Carver, Bradford, and the 15 men with them that the area around Plymouth Harbor was the best location to begin building a settlement. They noticed the cleared land in the area, crops seemed to have been grown, but there was no evidence of Native American dwellings. They saw an abundance of waterfowl, shellfish, and freshwater springs.

The men decided to take a closer look and walked through a cleared area. They were shocked to find human skulls and bones scattered on the surface of the ground. They could only conclude that people who lived there must have died over a short period – possibly murdered or perhaps contracting a disease that took them so quickly that the living were not able to bury the dead.

Bradford knew that food supplies on the Mayflower were running low, especially their store of beer. Passengers were increasingly sick. Some of the men with him in the exploration party were weak and unwell. He knew they could not expend more energy or time looking for other locations. They would let Master Jones and the passengers know they had found a site for a settlement. It would be called New Plymouth in honor of the port from which they last left England.

When the exploration party returned to the Mayflower in Provincetown Harbor, Bradford learned that his wife had fallen overboard. He was stoic in his acceptance of the news. Circumstances had become increasingly desperate. Grieving would come in time. Both John Carver and William Brewster embraced Bradford in silence. Tears flowed. Both Carver and Brewster thought of reminding Bradford of God's love and higher purpose, but no words were exchanged. For the time being, Bradford just needed to know through the closeness of an embrace that the men recognized the depth of his hurt.

On December 15th, responding to Bradford's recommendation, Master Jones directed that the Mayflower sail across Cape Cod Bay toward Plymouth Harbor. They arrived on the 18th. Mary Chilton's father, James, passed away before they reached their destination. Elisabeth and Desire sat with Mary, and at times cried with her.

Apart from Elisabeth and her teen friends and a few with whom they had shared hazelnuts – including Susanna White - passengers had had no supplement to their primary diet of salt pork, hardtack, and fish. Scurvy had set in. In combination with bitter cold and unsanitary conditions, half the passengers were seriously ill.

Chapter 34. New Plymouth: A Difficult Start

Men who had the strength to do so, made their way from the Mayflower to the shore to begin construction of the new settlement. Their first task was to build a communal structure for storage and sleeping. Trees were cut, and vertical trunks interwoven with branches to form walls. Clay and mud were pressed into the gaps to help keep out wind, rain, and snow. Reeds were woven together for a roof. Once a common structure was completed, the builders could stay overnight. Then the men from individual family groups could build their own houses.

Progress was slow because of cold, wetness, and the declining health of so many. Elisabeth, her friends, and other women remained on the Mayflower. As much as they wanted to be on land, they were needed on board to help care for the sick. No women would venture to shore until a shelter for sleeping was completed.

Elisabeth remembered the latter part of December 1620 and the first few months of 1621 as a horrific nightmare. Few days went by without someone dying. Even what might have been a momentarily happy diversion turned out not to be. Mary Allerton gave birth to a still-born son. Within weeks Mary herself would be buried.

Elisabeth saw her parents weaken and lose strength. She wondered if her Aunt Agnes and Uncle Edward would survive, and in fact, they did not. Both died in early January. Elisabeth's parents were soon to follow. Her mother was the first to die. Elisabeth knew her father would soon pass as well. Her father knew it too. While she sat beside him, he said quietly, "Elisabeth, are you there?"

"Yes, I'm here, father." He reached out and took hold of her hand.

"Do you remember when we looked through the telescope at the University in Leiden?"

"I'll never forget that, father. I think I'm the only girl who has seen Jupiter and its four moons."

She felt a slight squeeze from his hand.

"I'm so glad we could do that together," he said. "Your mother, Aunt Agnes, and Uncle Edward are in heaven, and I will join them soon. But you are strong and have much to do in this life. I must say this to you: The same God who put Jupiter and its moons and all the stars in the sky sees little sparrows and cares for them. He loves you even more and will sustain and provide for you – even when everything around you seems dark and difficult. Choose to trust Him, Dear, with the whole of your mind, will, and emotion."

Elisabeth was surprised at the intensity of her father's words. When he finished speaking, he slumped back in his blanket. She noticed his mouth was dry and said, "Father, I'm going to get you some beer." He smiled weakly at her. "Thank you, Elisabeth."

Within a few minutes, she returned with the drink. Her father was gone.

She had no idea how she could have survived such loss without the support of Desire, Mary, Constance, Priscilla, and Dorothy. They comforted one another and looked for ways to provide relief and solace to others. Despite watching loved ones die and seeing the overwhelming neediness of so many around them, the horror of specific circumstances did not crush their spirits.

Master Jones and his crew were kind to the girls and others who lost family members. Jones instructed his sailors to row passengers from the Mayflower to New Plymouth, where they could participate with Elder Brewster in nighttime burials. Most of the burials took place under cover of darkness because Governor Carver and military commander, Miles Standish, aware that Native Americans might be watching from the forest, did not want them to see how many of the passengers were dying. If Native Americans knew the weakness of the English, they might attack and kill everyone.

On one of their excursions from the ship to where men were building shelters, the girls learned that John Goodman had frozen his feet. He and Peter Browne had gone too far from the clearing to cut thatch for roofing and had become lost. They spent the night in freezing temperatures with inadequate clothing. While the men – and John's dogs – made it back to New Plymouth, John's feet were so swollen, others had to cut shoes from his feet.

Following the deaths of John and Joan Tilley, Katherine Carver invited Elisabeth to join their family group. "We would love to have you come and live with us, Elisabeth," Mrs. Carver said tenderly. Elisabeth knew her parents had high respect for the Carvers. In a very real way, there was not much of a decision for Elisabeth. At 13 – not quite 14 - she was too young to be on her own. And being with the Carver family meant she would spend more time with Desire Minter and Dorothy Jones, both of whom were already a part of Carvers' extended family.

Mary Chilton, whose parents had died, began to live with Susanna White. Susanna's husband William was very ill – soon to die – and Susanna needed support to look after infant son Peregrine and 6-year old son Resolved.

The process of moving remaining supplies and people off the Mayflower to the Plymouth settlement took place toward the end of January. Two communal shelters with thatched roofs were now completed, and work began on seven family homes. After the first communal structures were completed, individual families worked on their own houses. "We should use the same organizational pattern Nehemiah used in rebuilding Jerusalem," Elder William Brewster advised Governor Carver. "He directed citizens to build on their own property, knowing they would feel a greater sense of urgency when the building had personal meaning."

Governor Carver followed Brewster's advice. They found that the same strategy for construction worked well in Plymouth.

By the first of February, all passengers were off the Mayflower and living in the new community shelters. The building of family accommodations began, but fewer were needed because so many had died. Even though winter weather persisted through February, the fires within the shelters provided some comfort for both the sick and those who cared for them. Through the end of March 1621, 52 of the 102 Mayflower passengers died.

There were not many bright spots for Elisabeth, but one she always remembered was her first night sleeping in Plymouth. John Goodman's spaniel, Missy, came into the Carver house and lay down beside her. John Howland, also part of the Carver household, knew Goodman would be looking for Missy, but also knew Goodman's feet were still too sore to walk in search of the dog. "I'll let John Goodman know Missy is with you," Howland told Elisabeth. "He'll want to know she's safe."

Howland found Goodman to let him know Missy was sleeping beside Elisabeth. "I'm fine with that," said Goodman. "My feet are still so painful, I have a hard enough time looking after Sadie."

A number of Master Jones' crew members also became very sick, and several died. Jones was anxious to sail the Mayflower back to England but decided to delay leaving until sailors who were convalescing were well enough to perform their duties.

Chapter 35. Building a Settlement

By early March, the weather had warmed considerably. Governor Carver directed that unmarried men attach themselves to a family household, and work with that family so individual houses could be more quickly completed. John Howland, already a part of the Carver household, worked efficiently and effectively with the Governor. Their home was on the south side of what was to become the main street of town. They were the first to finish building a house after the larger communal shelters were completed.

The new buildings were much rougher than what settlers had known in England and Holland. But they were now home, and Elisabeth and her friends – along with everyone else - were glad to be away from the awful conditions on the Mayflower.

With the focus of life now ashore came a welcome change in diet. A few of the men were able to shoot ducks and geese from an abundance of waterfowl in the area. Roast duck and goose were a much-appreciated addition to the dwindling supplies remaining from the Mayflower. It was during a duck hunting expedition in mid-February that one of the men saw a group of Native Americans walk by just a short distance from where he was lying in the bushes. He lay very still, unseen until he felt it safe to return to the new townsite.

On hearing of the sighting, military leader Myles Standish, fearful of an imminent attack, sounded the alarm. All able-bodied men readied their rifles. No one had yet met face-to-face with a Native American, and both Standish and Governor Carver were uncertain whether a meeting would be friendly. No Natives were seen that day, but the

Governor urged everyone to be cautious and to stay close to the settlement.

Now that warmer weather had arrived, Mrs. Carver, Elisabeth, and Desire started the task of planting peas and barley seed brought from England. They planted peas behind their home on the 'main street' of Plymouth. The Brewster's property was on one side of the Carvers, and John Goodman's home on the other. Preparing the soil was not difficult because Native Americans had planted in the area a year or two earlier. Some of the men joined them to plant barley in a broader area further away from the houses.

On a warm afternoon at the beginning of the second week in March, Elisabeth and Missy went for a walk. Elisabeth intended to take a short hike around the plantation as she had done on several occasions already. Mr. Carver had said she could walk Missy, but to be sure to stay close enough to the buildings so she could get back quickly if she or Missy saw or heard any danger – danger that could have come from a wild animal or from Native Americans. Missy had a collar, but Elisabeth didn't like to keep her on a leash. Missy generally kept close to Elisabeth – unless, of course, the dog spotted something unusual.

On that afternoon, Missy and Elisabeth spotted the deer at the same time. They saw a doe and what looked to Elisabeth like a brand-new fawn. Missy and Elisabeth stopped in their tracks. Missy was initially very still, pressing against Elisabeth's leg. The doe spotted Elisabeth and Missy, and with her fawn, quickly leaped into the trees.

Movement by the deer was Missy's cue for pursuit. Her Springer spaniel heritage said a chase was on. Fearing she might lose Missy, Elisabeth ran in the direction the dog disappeared. She wasn't sure how far she ran after Missy. She didn't want to alarm Mr. Carver or others by shouting at the dog, but as she got further from the settlement, she knew she had to call out. Somehow Missy heard the panic in Elisabeth's voice and stopped chasing the deer. She trotted back toward Elisabeth, eyes bright, tail wagging, and tongue hanging out.

Elisabeth felt exhausted by her run. After being on the ship without much exercise for almost seven months, she was in no shape for vigorous exercise.

Elisabeth sat on a fallen tree to catch her breath, holding Missy's collar with one hand. She closed her eyes, breathing a prayer of thanksgiving that Missy came back, and hoping she would not get into trouble with Governor Carver for being out of sight of the settlement. Elisabeth wasn't sure how long she sat on the log with her eyes closed, but it was long enough for her breath to almost return to normal. She listened to the wind ripple lightly through the leaves in the trees around her. The snapping of a twig nearby startled her. Her eyes flashed open. Less than ten yards in front of her was a young girl, but unlike any she had ever seen. She wore a knee-length leather skirt and a cape around her shoulders. White quills decorated each shoulder of the cape. Long black hair was tied behind her neck. She wore moccasins that extended to the bottom of her dress. Her face was attractive. Both girls looked at each other, but neither seemed to be afraid. Even Missy, tail wagging, watched the girl and did not bark.

"Hello," said the young girl. "I am Hurit."

PART IV. HURIT'S STORY

Chapter 36. A Five-Day Journey

Hurit and her mother, Wawestseka, were preparing the evening meal of baked cod and boiled corn in their village on Pemaquid Point in present-day Maine. Sometimes they boiled the cod, but Hurit preferred it baked. Baking required the extra work of finding green birch bark for wrapping the cod so it could cook in the coals, but to Hurit, baked fish was so much more flavorful than boiled fish. Corn boiled in a clay pot.

A runner arrived as the meal was cooking. Runners brought communication from other tribes, and they always came to Hurit's home because her father, Samoset, was an Abenaki sagamore, a chief chosen by others in the band because they perceived him as wise, courageous, and confident.

Samoset and the runner talked for a short time outside the wetu, then both came in and sat on the blanketed floor. Samoset knew the runner. They had several times since Samoset accepted the position of sagamore. His name was Ahanu. He was a strong, trustworthy young man who had come as an emissary from Massasoit in Sowams, a five-day journey to the south. Massasoit needed advice from regional sagamores about the strategy he should take in dealing with a new group of Englishmen.

"They are different from any we've encountered before," was Ahanu's message from Massasoit.

"Tell me more about them," Samoset requested.

Ahanu continued, "These people are building houses in vacant Patuxet. Before they landed at Patuxet, they stole seed corn from the Nausets on Cape Cod. They have not approached any of our people for trade. It seems they have come to live. Women and children are with them. Massasoit says he will need you for two full moons – possibly more."

Massasoit recognized the value of input from others – and especially Samoset's wisdom. But he would also need Samoset's skill with the English language should there be a need to have direct communication with the English. Even though Squanto now lived in Massasoit's village and could speak English more fluently than could Samoset, Massasoit still wasn't confident he could trust Squanto.

Samoset had been to Sowams last spring and had talked with his old friend, Squanto. He learned that Squanto had returned to his home at Patuxet with Englishmen, who killed two of Massasoit's warriors. Squanto was captured during the altercation, and Massasoit did not trust him. Squanto pleaded with Samoset to intervene with Massasoit on his behalf so that he could be free, and though Samoset spoke with Massasoit on Squanto's behalf, Massasoit was not yet convinced. With his own eyes, he saw Squanto land and advance along the shore with English sailors. Something about Squanto did not feel right to Massasoit. However, both men recognized Squanto's fluency in English. It was clear he had mastered the language. If his heart were true, perhaps Massasoit would find Squanto's skill in speaking English to be useful in the near future.

There was no question about whether Samoset would go to Sowams to talk with Massasoit and share his insights. But he was not prepared for Hurit's question to him in the morning.

"Father, you will be away for a long time. I could keep you company and learn much if I were to go with you. You know how I like to make new friends. May I go?"

The statements and question delighted Samoset. His daughter actually wanted to be with him – her father! But he knew that for Hurit to go with him, Wawestseka would need to feel good about it. He motioned to Wawestseka to come with him. Hurit knew she should stay behind. Samoset and his wife walked in silence for several minutes. They paused in a clearing that overlooked the ocean. Wawestseka turned to her husband and said,

"I heard Hurit's question. It is wonderful that our daughter wants to go with you on this journey. You must take her. She will not live in our home for long. Before we know it, one of our young men will take her to a new abode."

"What will you do while we're gone?" asked Samoset.

"I will be with my parents and yours," said Wawestseka. "It will be good for all of us."

"Thank you, my beautiful one," responded Samoset. "I too am glad Hurit wants to come with me. If ever there is a good time for her to be along, this trip might be it. If the English have children with them, they are more likely to want peace than war, so the danger for her will be less."

And so it was that Hurit and her father embarked on a five-day journey to Sowams. "Look carefully at the hills and streams, trees, and where the sun, moon, and stars are," he told Hurit. "I fully expect we will come back together, but if something should happen to me, I want you to be able to find your way home." Hurit's father also pointed out specific landmarks along their route.

During the journey, Hurit recalled the evenings she sat with her father and other men around fires, talking about the English sailors they met, and how her father had conversed with them. "Father," said Hurit, "tell me again about the English words and customs you learned when you talked with the sailors from the floating islands."

Occasionally when she had spent time with her father in the past, he pronounced English words he had learned and explained what they meant. Hurit repeated what she heard her father say, and at one time, he laughed, saying, "I have the only daughter among our people who can speak English."

Their current conversation about language reminded Samoset of his old traveling companion, Squanto, now under house arrest in Massasoit's town of Sowams. "My friend and I sure had some interesting times trying to communicate with English sailing captains," he said to Hurit. He then recalled again for her some of the basics of what he knew of the English language. "They wanted to know my name, where I lived, how many people lived in the area, what we ate, what kinds of animals were in the area. Sometimes Squanto and I could only make motions to communicate what we thought they were asking. Specific words were not always easy to distinguish."

"And," he continued, "the English always told us about their great King, King James - about his great power and his keen interest in our lands."

On day five, Samoset and his daughter arrived at Sowams. Massasoit welcomed them warmly. His home was spacious, and they stayed there with him. Massasoit told Samoset about what his men and other bands in the region had observed about the English group now at Patuxet – from the time of arrival at the northern tip of Cape Cod and stealing corn from the Nausets, to excursions around the bay in a smaller boat, taking a few days to explore Patuxet, returning to the great ship, bringing it across the bay, constructing houses at Patuxet, and noticing that many had died.

He spoke of seeing mostly men comprising the English group but observed that women and children were with them. Their ship, the floating island, was still at rest in the bay. They had a smaller boat for sailing close to shore and a smaller boat yet having no sail.

"Some of my men have set up wetu in a camp close to Patuxet," said Massasoit. "They are watching the movements of the English closely to better understand their purpose. My instinct tells me to beware, but I would like your counsel about whether we should consider the new people to be friends or foes. Should we drive them away from our land, or could they be allies to strengthen our hand in dealing with other tribes who would do us harm?"

"I would like to get a close look at what they are doing," said Samoset. "I will go to your camp for a few days and scout the English at Patuxet to see for myself."

Samoset intended to go to the camp near Patuxet by himself, leaving Hurit with Massasoit's family. However, she was insistent. "My eyes and ears are good, father, and I am almost as fleet of foot as you are. I'm here with you, and I would like to see the English. You've told me so much about them."

Samoset smiled at his daughter and said, "You are as persistent and persuasive as your mother! Yes, you may come, but I need you to promise to do exactly as I tell you. If anything bad should happen to you, I could never forgive myself!"

The next day Samoset and Hurit left Massasoit's home, accompanied by two of his warriors. Their purpose was to observe the English from a distance, then return to Sowams to report their findings to Massasoit.

Chapter 37. The First Meeting

Hurit's father and mother had a signal they often used to call Hurit when they didn't know precisely where she was. Both parents were able to whistle in a way that sounded like a veery, a small, sparrow-like bird having a loud distinctive song with three repeated notes. When Hurit heard the signal, she knew it was essential to come toward the sound to find her mother or her father.

Today as she and her father and the two men left their camp to view the English settlement, Samoset reminded Hurit of the signal. "We must be cautious," he said. "When you hear me whistle the call of the veery, look carefully all around you, and then if it is safe, come towards my call as quickly and quietly as you can."

"Yes, father, I will," she replied. Hurit felt excitement at the prospect of seeing English people. "I wonder what the children are like?" she thought.

As the group neared the site where the English were building houses, they split up, with Hurit and her father moving to circle around the north side, and the other two men circling around the south side. Hurit was used to walking quietly through the forest. She had been with her father on hunting trips and knew how essential soundless movement could be. Today was particularly critical for stealth. They wanted to observe the English settlers without being seen – as Massasoit's men had done throughout the winter.

On the crest of a small hill, Samoset stopped and quickly put his hand on Hurit's shoulder. "I see the houses," he whispered. Hurit inched forward until she too could see the houses and building activity over the crest of the hill. They both noticed how different the houses were from their wetu. These houses were angular, rather than rounded.

"Let's go a bit further," said Samoset. They circled further until they were almost directly north of the building site. "Wait here for me," he said. "I'm going down the hill to get a view from the ocean side. Be sure to stay quiet and out of view. I won't be long."

"Ok Father," she responded quietly. Her father slipped away silently. She was always impressed with how quickly and quietly he moved. If she did not see him, she would not have known he was there.

Not long after her father had disappeared down the hill, she spotted a doe slightly closer to the houses than where her father had gone downhill toward the ocean. Nearby, a fawn was curled up. Hurit guessed the fawn was not more than a day old. At almost the same time, she saw a girl – what must be an English girl - and a dog walking in her direction. The girl had long, light brown hair. She wore a long dark dress and a light-colored coat and hat. The dog was the most beautiful dog Hurit had ever seen: mostly white with red markings, and short fur. Hurit watched intently as the pair came toward the doe and fawn. She moved below the crest of the hill to be sure she was out of sight. She paused for a few moments listening carefully, then heard a crackling of twigs and rustling of dead leaves. She guessed that the doe must have been frightened and bounded away. She hoped the fawn's legs were strong enough to keep up with its mother.

Hurit edged back to the crest of the hill to see what was happening. The doe and fawn were gone, and the English girl was running in the direction they must have disappeared. The dog had disappeared as well, probably chasing the deer. She heard the girl give several panicked calls – perhaps for the dog. Hurit was amazed that the dog returned to the girl. The girl knelt by the dog and put her arms around it. After a short time, she sat on a log that was at an angle to Hurit's location. She continued to hold on to something around the dog's neck. Hurit could tell the girl was out of breath.

Keeping below the crest of the hill, Hurit, circled toward where she saw the girl sit. When she peered again over the edge, the girl and her dog were closer than she thought. Hurit could see the girl's eyes were closed, and she seemed to still be breathing quite heavily. Hurit noticed that their location was out of the line of sight of the buildings. Almost without thinking, she stepped quietly over the crest of the hill. Keeping behind trees as best she could, she moved silently toward the girl. About ten yards away, she stopped. The dog saw her, and much to Hurit's relief did not bark or attack. For a moment, the dog's tail stopped wagging. Then the dog, still looking at Hurit, pushed closer to the girl, tail wagging again. What a beautiful dog, Hurit thought. It had droopy ears and such beautiful coloration.

The girl opened her eyes and looked at the dog. "Thank you, Missy," she said. Then noticing the dog was focused on something else, Elisabeth looked in the direction in which the dog was fixated. She saw Hurit. Hurit could see the surprise on her face. At first, neither girl said anything. Then Hurit remembered what her father had said when he introduced himself to English sailors. With a smile on her face, she pointed to herself and said to the girl, "I am Hurit."

The girl looked even more surprised, but soon a smile came to her face. She finally found her voice and responded, "Hello, Hurit. I am Elisabeth."

"I must get back to the houses or men will come looking for me," said Elisabeth, pointing toward the settlement. She wasn't sure whether Hurit understood. The girls smiled warmly at one another, and Elisabeth, with one hand remaining on Missy's collar, turned to walk away. "I will come again to visit," said Hurit, remembering the conversation she had practiced with her father. Elisabeth noticed the dark, intense, and bright eyes of the girl. She knew she wanted to learn much more about her. "I hope we can meet again soon," Elisabeth said. She heard the concerns expressed by the men about the danger the

Native Americans posed and didn't know if or when another meeting would even be possible.

Hurit melted back into the forest, beneath the crest of the hill. She could hardly believe she had met and talked to an English girl! And she knew the girl's name: Elisabeth. She wondered when another meeting might be possible. The sound of a veery interrupted her thoughts. To the right, up a slight rise, she heard, then saw her father.

He had a look of concern on his face. "I heard the English girl call," said her father. "Panic was in her voice, and I thought you might be in danger. You let her see you. That could have been very dangerous for us both! I'm glad you're safe – but why did you do that?"

Hurit heard the scolding in her father's voice. Tears came to her eyes, "I didn't think of the danger," said Hurit. "I just wanted to meet an English girl."

"Did you try to say anything to the girl?" asked her father.

"I told the girl my name using the words you told me about when you introduced yourself to the English sailors. She told me her name and said something else. I think she and her dog were going back to their village."

"We must move swiftly," said Samoset. "When she tells others what she saw, they will be out here quickly looking for us, and we could be in great danger."

Father and daughter walked quietly but quickly back toward the camp where they had spent the night. Both maintained a watchfulness of their surroundings, and both wondered about the English people: Hurit wondering about the English girl and her beautiful dog; Samoset was relieved that the English had not seen them and wondering how relationships with these new people would develop. After observing the brief meeting between his daughter and the English girl, he hoped relations could be peaceful.

PART V. COMING TOGETHER

Chapter 38. A Strategic Second Meeting

Back at the village of Sowams, Massasoit listened to counsel from Samoset and other sagamores who he had brought together for advice. He felt many forces at play. There was pressure from the Narragansett tribe to the south. Massasoit knew they would attempt to coerce tribute from his Wampanoag people if they thought themselves stronger. Because of recent sickness and death of many of the people he governed, he knew his strength in battle would be limited.

The English could potentially be allies, but Massasoit did not yet know if he could trust them. While some English had come in ships and traded fairly, others came and kidnapped or killed. Were the English now building houses at Patuxet trustworthy? Their weapons were fearsome. Even a few English guns would be difficult for his men to overcome with bows and arrows. However, if the English turned out to be honorable, an alliance with them could establish greater security for his people and almost certainly discourage an attack from the Narragansetts.

Opinions on all issues were vigorously expressed as sagamores conveyed their views. Massasoit appreciated the diverse viewpoints, but no individual perspective stood out as being the best path forward. Finally, he turned to Samoset and said, "You speak the language of the English. I would like you to go to their village. Talk with them in their new settlement to get a sense of their intentions. Find out what they want. We will not find peace through force. Perhaps we can find it with them through communication and understanding. If it turns out that peace is not an option, we will drive them from our land. After you have observed and talked, come back and report what you learn."

"A wise step forward, Massasoit," said Samoset. "I am glad to go to talk with the English."

Massasoit and his advisory group were strategic in helping Samoset plan his visit. They wanted him to interact with the English in a way that would be disarming, yet cause them to think carefully about their own actions. The planning group came up with the idea of Samoset initiating a friendly meeting, yet taking with him a bow and quiver – the quiver having just two arrows: one with a sharp, deadly arrowhead, and the other with no arrowhead at all. The English would experience Samoset's friendly contact. Surely they would understand that the arrow with no tip represented peace while the one with a barbed arrowhead meant war. The advisory group wanted the English to carefully consider the choice they faced: peace on one hand, or hostilities on the other hand. The decision about war or peace would be theirs. Massasoit need issue no threat.

A second element of strategic planning was for Samoset to decide whether his English skills were sufficient, or whether there was a need to engage Squanto in communication. Squanto's English skills were excellent, but Massasoit and some of his advisors were not sure where his loyalty lay. Samoset would determine the need for Squanto's expertise based on the degree to which he understood what the English communicated and whether the English indicated a desire for peace. If greater fluency was needed, Massasoit would consider releasing Squanto from what was essentially a house arrest in the village and allow him to accompany Samoset on a subsequent visit. Or, if the English chose war, Squanto's assistance would not be needed.

A third element of the strategic plan was to gauge the interest of the English in meeting with Massasoit – should peace be their choice. What questions did they ask? Were they interested in trade? Did they show interest in meeting with a leader?

On March 16th, 1621, Samoset returned to Patuxet – now called Plymouth by the English. Hurit did not accompany her father this time. "Let's see how my contact turns out," he told her. "This first visit with the English is too risky for you to come with me."

Samoset decided to begin the visit with as much surprise as possible. He moved silently through the trees, emerging into a clearing at Plymouth as close as possible to the buildings under construction. Samoset strode boldly and confidently toward the English. His strides were long and purposeful. He saw some men scramble to pick up guns, but no rifles were pointed at him. As he came closer to the structures, he noticed the women and children hurry toward the largest structure. Among them was the young girl he had seen with Hurit. She and her dog stood at the entrance to the building. As he came closer, he noticed she looked straight into his eyes. Perhaps greeting the young girl might be the place to start.

As he was about to say hello to Elisabeth, several men stepped into his way. He stopped, raised his hand, and with a disarming smile, said to them, "Welcome, Englishmen!"

The men were shocked, and for a short time, speechless. After all the concern they felt about hostilities, and their fear of being watched, a Native American was in their midst, greeting them in English no less! He was much taller than all of the Englishmen, except perhaps for John Howland. They marveled at his well-developed physique. Somewhat disconcerting was the fact that he was naked except for a fringed deerskin loin covering. How could he not be cold? All of them were wearing coats and pants. One of the men, thinking Samoset might be cold, threw a cloak around his shoulders.

Samoset's next words were, "I'd like some beer."

"Of course! Welcome to Plymouth, my friend," said Governor Carver. "Come sit with me. "Howland, please bring us nourishment."

Governor Carver, William Brewster, and several other men guided Samoset to one of the buildings where they sat together. John knew their supply of beer was dwindling, so he brought Samoset a cup of brandy and some roasted duck. When Samoset finished the drink and food, he introduced himself and told the men in his limited English where he was from. He told about the people on whose land the English were now building. "All who lived here died of a sickness," he said. "Only one man survived. You may meet him soon."

The conversation continued back and forth until sunset. The English had many questions about the area: What people live nearby? What animals are in the area? Were furs available for trade? What crops are grown? What would you like in trade for furs? Is it possible for us to live here in peace? Can we meet with your leader? Samoset understood some of the questions, but soon realized it would be necessary for his friend Squanto to help with communication.

As evening approached, the English hoped Samoset would leave, but he did not. Finally, Stephen Hopkins volunteered to have Samoset stay with his family in the home he had recently completed. It had been less than six weeks since two-year-old daughter Damaris, and infant son Oceanus had passed away. Still somewhat uncertain about the intentions of their guest, Stephen, his wife Elisabeth, 14-year old Constance, and 12-year old Giles slept lightly that night. Samoset slept soundly.

In the morning, Samoset enjoyed left-over roast duck with the men. He told them he would like to bring his leader, Massasoit, to continue the conversation they had started last night. "Of course! Yes, we would be honored to meet with Massasoit and talk with him," said Governor Carver.

"I will be back in six days," said Samoset, "and Massasoit will come with me."

As he was leaving, Samoset noticed Elisabeth and Missy in the doorway of a nearby house. "Hurit was pleased to meet you and your dog," he said. Elisabeth was delighted to hear Samoset's words. She smiled and was pleasantly surprised at the strength in her voice as she said, "Thank you, Sir. Tell Hurit I would like to see her again."

"She will come with me in six days," he responded. With that, Samoset strode across the clearing and disappeared into the forest.

The English were left, staring after Samoset. "Can you believe what just happened?" Governor Carver said to those standing near him. No one responded. They just shook their heads.

Chapter 39. The Agreement

Samoset's message to Massasoit and his advisory group was threefold: the English would prefer peace and trade with Native Americans rather than hostilities; they would like to meet Massasoit; and Squanto was needed to help with clear communication between the groups.

Samoset also told the advisory group about Hurit's unanticipated meeting with the English girl. The improbable encounter of the two girls may have been a valuable introduction. If children were friendly, perhaps that would influence the adults.

Massasoit was deep in thought for a few moments. Then looking around the circle of men gathered with him, he said, "Peace and war begin in our minds. We will first try the path of peace. If an alliance with the English works, it will protect us from domination by the Narragansets. If the English want to trade, what we acquire from them will strengthen our position in this region."

He directed that women and children accompany the men to meet the English. They should be prepared to escape quickly if hostilities arise. Perhaps as Samoset suggested, the presence of women and children would prompt the English to also choose a peaceful path forward. Massasoit was all too aware that the population of his band was already depleted due to a plague in the recent past. War would only take more of his people.

However, Massasoit did not want to appear to the English to be weak on this first visit. "We will also go in strength," he said. "Our warriors must be prepared for combat." Like the contrast provided by the two arrows Samoset took on his first visit, the presence of the women and children would contrast with battle-ready warriors causing the English to think carefully about their response.

Six days later, on March 22nd, 1621, Samoset returned to Plymouth with his old friend, Squanto. It felt good to them both to once again be traveling together. Hurit was with them. Not far behind on the journey was Massasoit, with 60 battle-ready warriors. Accompanying them were their wives and children. They would set up a temporary camp within a short distance of Plymouth in preparation for meeting the English.

On this occasion, Samoset, Hurit, Squanto, and two additional warriors strode boldly into the village. To say that the day was a day of surprises for the English would be as much of an understatement as saying they had experienced minor difficulties on their voyage across the ocean.

The English were surprised – again – at the boldness of the Native Americans. They arrived when they said they would; they showed absolutely no fear, striding boldly into the English camp, even daring to bring a young girl. Some of the English still questioned whether Elisabeth really had met a Native American girl, or whether what she told them was part of an active imagination. It was evident by how she and Hurit greeted one another that they had already met. Even Missy seemed glad to see Hurit again. Elisabeth immediately invited Hurit to come with her to meet her English friends, Desire, Mary, Constance, Priscilla, and Dorothy.

Next, the English were shocked by the excellence of Squanto's English and stunned to learn he had lived in England. He recounted for them about living in Spain, traveling with Master Slany, residing in the Cornhill area of London, meeting Sir Walter Raleigh, attending a play at the Globe theater, meeting King James, and working in Newfoundland. It seemed he had done more things, met more highly placed people, and traveled more than most of them had. And he repeated what Samoset had told them - that they were now building a village at the very site where he had once lived before he and others were kidnapped by Captain Hunt. Because of a plague that occurred during his absence, everyone who lived in his village had died.

The next shock came while they were still listening to Squanto. A Native American they soon learned was Massasoit, stepped out of the trees on the southwest of the clearing. His face was painted red, and he looked absolutely fearsome. He was taller than Samoset and had a similar well-developed physique. Not far behind him were at least 60 warriors whose faces were also painted various colors: some red, some white, some black, some yellow. They appeared ready for war. The English could hardly believe what they were seeing!

Governor Carver was first to recover from the shock of such a fearsome sight, directing Edward Winslow to take a gift and go out to meet Massasoit. Carver needed time to prepare for the meeting with Massasoit within the settlement. Winslow quickly found a gift of food, brandy, and a knife, and strode out to meet Massasoit. Massasoit was pleased with the offering. Winslow indicated that Massasoit should advance to the settlement with a few of his warriors while he, Winslow, stayed with the rest of Massasoit warriors at the edge of the clearing.

Meanwhile, John Howland spread a blanket on the floor within one of the houses. He also readied strong water, or brandy, to serve their guest. Governor Carver was now ready to meet with Massasoit.

The meeting between Massasoit and Governor Carver went well. It was a scene the Governor and his associates had not imagined: a fearsome-looking, tall, well-built Native American Chief and his equally fearsome looking, well-built advisors sitting with the much smaller, frail-looking Governor Carver and his advisors, all of whom looked equally frail.

In another part of the settlement, Elisabeth, Desire, Mary, Constance, Priscilla, and Dorothy did their best to converse with Hurit. Missy sat with them, tail wagging, feeling good to be part of the group. Elisabeth thought back to when she first met Rembrandt and the initial awkwardness of learning to converse with him in Dutch. It would be a challenge to learn to communicate with Hurit, but she knew she could do it and was determined to do so.

The men, aided by Squanto as their interpreter, made rapid progress. They negotiated an agreement of peace and cooperation before the end of the day.

The girls, having no interpreter, had more difficulty communicating, but it was clear that each of the English girls was delighted to meet Hurit, and wanted to learn more about her. They all touched her deerskin clothing. It felt soft and looked so much more comfortable than their long, flowing skirts. They loved the black and white porcupine quills that decorated Hurit's buckskin top and her hair.

They could see that Hurit carried herself with confidence. If she felt fear or uncomfortable, it was not evident. She tried very hard to communicate with them using English words she had learned from her father.

After reaching a peace agreement with the English, Massasoit and his warriors returned to their temporary camp near Plymouth to be with their wives and children. Samoset and Squanto slept in the home of the Winslow family. Hurit stayed with Elisabeth and Missy in the Carver household.

Chapter 40. Transitions

Governor Carver was so pleased with Squanto's help with communication and knowledge of the area that he asked Massasoit if Squanto could remain in Plymouth. Massasoit was still uncertain of where Squanto's loyalty lay. However, the new agreement with the English stated that an individual from one group who dealt treacherously with the other group would be handed over for appropriate punishment. Massasoit decided it would be best for everyone if Squanto stayed with the English.

For his part, Squanto was grateful for renewed freedom and the opportunity to live where his home had once been. He knew his time with the English in Plymouth could become a strong position of influence for him, and possibly one of power. He had a good understanding of English and Native American cultures, and he would effectively control the communication between the two groups. He had not consciously sought this position. Circumstances beyond his control brought him here. He knew he did not enjoy his time as a prisoner or slave. Living with the English in their new settlement could be the start of something much better.

An additional part of Squanto's responsibility was to help the English with their food sources. He would show them how to plant the Native American crops of corn, squash, and beans. The peas and barley the English had brought from England and planted were growing, but not doing nearly as well as they had hoped. Additional crops would be needed for survival. The work of farming in Native American culture was mostly women's work, but Squanto had observed enough – and at times helped – so that he knew how it was done. He would also show the English how to fish more effectively, gather eels from the mud, and harvest shellfish and lobsters.

Samoset and Hurit returned to Sowams with Massasoit. They would stay there for at least another month until Massasoit knew with some confidence that the new agreement with the English was working.

On April 5th, Master Jones and his crew raised the anchor of the Mayflower in Plymouth Harbor and began the voyage back to England. All the surviving passengers gathered on the slope of the hill at Plymouth to watch the ship leave. Feelings were indeed mixed. Most were glad they did not have to return with the ship. It had been a horrendous crossing coming to their new home. They had had quite enough of seasickness and the vile conditions on board. However, the ship's leaving meant that Master Jones' support was gone, as was their link to home. No one knew when another ship from England would return. They were truly on their own.

Fifty people remained alive of the 102 passengers who started out from England. They would have to find a way to survive. And their dream was to be more than survivors. Governor Carver and his band of Separatists aspired to live as a spiritual community, and beyond that to thrive alongside Strangers – those who did not share their religious beliefs – as a business community that was politically stable, financially viable, and in harmony with their environment.

Squanto was, in large part, responsible for the survival of the English beyond those first few months. He showed how to use fish heads and even whole fish to fertilizer each seed. Elisabeth could not help but observe how planting and fishing were so closely linked. It was the first of many insights she gained about what, at first, seemed like improbable connections throughout nature.

The work of planting took considerable time and energy. Everyone pitched in to help, including Governor Carver. In the week after the Mayflower had left Plymouth Harbor, the Governor suffered heatstroke. Perhaps he had wanted to set an example for others with his strong work ethic. Whatever the motivation, he remained too long in the hot sun.

At first, he felt some muscle cramps and slight dizziness but continued with planting. His dizziness increased, and his headache progressed quickly from mild to severe. His wife, Katherine, finally noticed his distress and insisted he get out of the sun. She guided him to their home to lie down. Back at his house, Governor Carver lay down but soon fell into a coma. His body was too weak to recover. Within two days, he died.

Mrs. Carver did not talk much to others, but she confided in the three young girls living in her household at the time, Elisabeth, Desire, and Dorothy, that she felt responsible for her husband's death. "I should have done more for him," she told them. "If I had brought him out of the sun sooner, I know he would not have died."

The girls did their best to reassure and encourage Mrs. Carver, but a deep depression set in. Elisabeth, Desire, and Dorothy took on her responsibilities in the home. Some said later that Mrs. Carver simply wanted to be with her husband. It seemed that she just gave up on life. Within a month, she too passed away.

For the six teenaged girls who came on the Mayflower, it had been a grim winter. Elisabeth had seen six adults close to her die: first her aunt and uncle; then both her parents. Now the Carvers who served for a short time as her stepparents, both passed away.

Both of Mary Chilton's parents died.

Priscilla Mullins' parents and younger brother died.

Constance Hopkins' 2-year old sister and infant brother died.

Desire Minter and Dorothy Jones, both living in the Carver household, lost the two adults closest to them.

As often as chores in the village and work of survival allowed, the girls spent time together to talk and confide their feelings about what was happening around them. Still, in their teens, they had experienced more loss and death in the past six months than most people experience in a lifetime. Their conversations helped reaffirm that they were not at fault for the many deaths. They had done as much as possible to ease the suffering and pain of loved ones.

Their talks also helped them recognize that nothing they could do would bring back those who died. They needed to look to the future and focus on what they could be grateful for from day to day. They had the friendship and support of one another, and despite the harshness of their environment, rugged beauty surrounded them.

Their discussions supported and reaffirmed their belief that the ultimate source for security came from their Creator. Though they had many questions about life, death, and the ongoing hardships they faced, they believed the Creator of the heavens and earth would provide their needs.

A comment Desire made caused Elisabeth to remember her father's parting words. Desire had said, "We care for our sheep and pigs and chickens each day, making sure they have the food and water they need. God will do that and more for us, including giving us the strength to face each day." Elisabeth recalled for the girls the visit she and her father made to the university in Leiden – and her father's last words to her, "The same God who put Jupiter and its moons and all the stars in the sky, sees little sparrows and cares for them. He loves you even more, and will provide for you."

The deaths within the community had practical impacts on life. Governor Carver's death meant that a new governor was needed. William Bradford seemed the logical choice. A vote by show of hands was carried out. The question was, "are you willing for William Bradford to serve as Governor?" All those present raised their hands, and Bradford became the new Governor.

One of his first tasks was to marry Edward Winslow and Susanna White. Separatists saw no evidence of church weddings in the Bible, so no pastor was needed for such ceremonies. Marriages were civil affairs at which the Governor officiated.

At first glance, the coming together of Edward and Susanna seemed to be simply a marriage of convenience. Both had lost their spouses shortly after their arrival at Plymouth. Susanna had the added burden of 4-month old son Peregrine and 6-year old son Resolved. In early May of 1621, they recognized one another's needs, saw how they could support one another, and on May 12th became the first couple in Plymouth to marry. Whatever their initial reasons for marriage, love between them grew and blossomed.

Mary Chilton moved with Susanna into the Winslow household to continue helping with baby Peregrine and young Resolved.

Chapter 41. A Visit to Hurit's Home

On their way home to Pemaquid Point in mid-May, Samoset and Hurit stopped in Plymouth. They arrived in late afternoon, and Governor Bradford invited them to stay overnight. Around the fire in the early evening, Elisabeth sat with Hurit on her left. To her right was Squanto. To Hurit's left was her father, Samoset. Elisabeth appreciated Squanto's presence around the fire because his being there made the conversation between herself and Hurit flow much better – even though they both did their best to learn words and phrases in each other's language. Whenever they were stuck on how to say a word or express a thought, Squanto was able to help.

The thrust of their conversation that evening went something like this. "My father and I need to go to our home," said Hurit. "In three full moons, my father must return to meet with Massasoit and his advisors. I would like you to come with my father and me to see our home and how we live. You can come back to Plymouth with us when we return."

Elisabeth's first thought was, "What an adventure that would be!" and then "No, I can't leave my friends and family here." Almost as quickly as those thoughts went through her mind, she realized she had no family to talk to or request permission for such an adventure. Tears briefly came to her eyes. Each of her teen friends was involved in supporting other families. Only John Howland remained in the Carver household, and he really didn't need her help. He could certainly look after himself, and anyway, she spent most of her time at the Brewsters' home now.

After those thoughts had flashed through her mind, Elisabeth responded to Hurit, "I would love the adventure of coming to visit your home, Hurit. What does your father think?"

"My father thinks we could learn much from one another," Hurit responded. "I already talked with him about your coming with us during our walk from Sowams. If you come, we could practice one another's language, you could learn how we live and cook, my mother and I could show you how we make buckskin clothing, and you could teach us to knit with your wool."

"Would it be ok if I brought Missy along?" asked Elisabeth.

"Yes," responded Hurit. "My father and I talked about that too, and he agreed."

Elisabeth looked over at Hurit's father, and asked, "Will you and Squanto come with Hurit and me to talk with Governor Bradford to ask about my going?"

The men nodded and smiled. "We'll come," Samoset said.

Samoset, Squanto, and the two girls walked over to where Governor Bradford was seated. When he heard the request, he asked William Brewster and Edward Winslow to join him: William Brewster because Elisabeth was now living in the Brewster household; and Edward Winslow because of his background in working with Native Americans in Virginia. Initially, all three men rejected the idea of a young English girl leaving to live with a Native American family. Would they ever see her again? Was this an attempt to steal one of their own children? However, Squanto intervened and was persuasive with his arguments. He convinced the men that friendship between the girls would be seen by bands in the region in a broader context of friendship between Native Americans and the English. "It will benefit all our people to see friendship between our children and your children," he said, then added, "the girls could learn much from one another. And I, Squanto, will personally guarantee her return to Plymouth in three full moons, before the colors of the leaves change."

Bradford, Brewster, and Winslow were persuaded by Squanto's arguments and accepted his word guaranteeing her return. They also recognized the losses young Elisabeth had experienced – indeed, her losses were as great as anyone had experienced since the beginning of the journey from Leiden. Perhaps a few months away in a different environment would aid the healing of her spirit.

Elisabeth was excited about the adventure that lay ahead with Hurit and her family. She had little to pack – one change of clothes, eight skeins of wool and a set of knitting needles, all which Samoset placed in the pack he carried. Elisabeth also brought along her gratefulness journal.

Elisabeth's teen friends were happy for her because they could see her excitement about going with Hurit. John Goodman gave his blessing for Elisabeth to take Missy. Early the next morning, Elisabeth hugged each of the girls, said goodbye to the Brewsters and John Howland, and left Plymouth with Missy, Hurit, and Samoset.

It was a long, five-day trek to Pemaquid Point, but Elisabeth thoroughly enjoyed it. The weather was beautiful, and she drank in the splendor of the forest. Sometimes she and Hurit conversed, and sometimes they just enjoyed walking in silence. She wondered out loud how Samoset knew the way without getting lost.

"Mostly the sun tells me the right direction," he said, "and the stars tell me that at night. Day and night I listen for the sound of the ocean and look for where the sun rises. When the sun and stars are hidden by clouds, we sometimes need other markers." He pointed to a tree that had part of its trunk growing sideways. "When that tree was young, one of our elders bent the tree over, tied a length of rawhide to the upper part of the tree, and used a rock to hold the tree so that it stayed bent. As the tree grew, the bend became a permanent part of the growing tree, and it serves to mark our path."

Elisabeth picked up on some Abenaki words and phrases quite quickly. She felt fortunate that Samoset could help translate and explain much of what she did not understand. She could tell that the language learning process would be less problematic than what she had experienced in learning Dutch with Rembrandt in Leiden. And Elisabeth could tell Missy thought this journey through the forest must be something like dog heaven.

It was touching to watch Hurit and her father reunite with Hurit's mother, Wawestseka. She saw a mixture of laughter, tears, and long hugs. She understood very little of what was said because it seemed they talked so fast. Finally, Hurit introduced Elisabeth. Wawestseka smiled warmly and gave Elisabeth an affectionate hug. She said something to Hurit that Elisabeth didn't understand. Elisabeth looked inquiringly at Samoset who, smiled and said, "My wife would like to get you into some more practical clothes." Elisabeth smiled broadly. She knew that meant a buckskin dress, and she looked forward to wearing one. "Tell Wawestseka I would be glad to be dressed like Hurit," said Elisabeth.

The family sat outside in the early evening sun. Elisabeth listened to Hurit tell her mother about her experiences in Sowams and Plymouth, about how she had first met Elisabeth and Missy, and about staying overnight in an English home. From time to time, Elisabeth would look inquisitively at Samoset. He gave her a summary of what was being said, and occasionally would explain an Abenaki word or phrase.

Neighbors heard about the girl with the strange clothes and beautiful dog and came by to look at Elisabeth and Missy. While she knew she looked different from Native American girls, Elisabeth did not feel at all embarrassed. She had confidence in who she was and felt very much accepted by Hurit and her family. There was nothing she could do about her clothing at the moment. However, she looked forward to exchanging her current apparel for a buckskin dress.

Hurit's home had about the same amount of space inside as the house the Carvers had built. The most significant difference was the rounded shape of Hurit's home. It was about 14 feet in circumference. The highest point was over eight feet above the ground. At that point, there was an opening in the center at the top. Elisabeth noticed that clay pots were used for cooking rather than metal pots she was used to.

The days and weeks passed quickly. Each day brought a new adventure and fascinating tasks. Some days Hurit and Elisabeth were with Wawestseka, and other days the two girls accompanied Samoset. No matter where adventures took Elisabeth, Missy was her constant companion.

Alongside Wawestseka, the girls helped with cooking. They also assisted the preparation of deer hides, from the scraping process to tanning of hides with a boiled paste, to smoking the hides over an open fire to help with waterproofing. Some hides were used for clothing and moccasins. Others were used for coverings on the inside and outside of the walls of wetu. Elisabeth was fascinated by the different plants and plant parts that Wawestseka assembled for dyeing. Roots, bark, and flowers all served for various colors. Porcupine quills added beautiful decoration. They looked attractive as part of the ornamentation on clothing and hair, but Elisabeth soon found out how painful they could be when one of the quills pricked her finger.

With Samoset, the girls helped prepare other animal skins such as beaver for use as clothing or for trade. They also helped Samoset gather fish from traps in the river, eels from the mudflats, and lobsters and clams from the ocean. Elisabeth noticed that overall, women focused on tasks related to apparel, tending crops, and cooking while men's duties had more to do with hunting, food gathering, and trade. Both men and women shared in the task of maintaining their home.

After supper one evening, Hurit asked her father to tell the story of how he asked her mother to become his wife. Samoset laughed and related the story while the family sat around the fire. "At the time of corn harvest," he said "there is a legend that says if a young man finds a red ear of corn, he may ask a young woman of his choosing for a kiss. If she accepts, it is a public declaration of their love for one another. I knew Wawestseka was the one for me, but I had not been bold enough to talk about marriage with her father. During that harvest season, I searched the corn plants until I found an ear of red corn. Discovering it provided the opportunity to ask for a kiss and let her know my feelings for her. When I asked for a kiss, Wawestseka said, 'Yes.' After our kiss, she looked deeply into my eyes, and with a smile that made by heart leap said, 'Thank you, Samoset, but what took you so long to ask?'"

Samoset looked over at Wawestseka. Their eyes met, and both had a hearty laugh. Elisabeth could tell that Hurit's parents were very much in love. "I'm glad it was you and not some of those other boys who found the ear of red corn," said Wawestseka.

Samoset got up from his seat by the fire to respond to a query from another member of the community. As he did so, Elisabeth listened as Wawestseka turned to Hurit in a more serious tone and said, "Your father is highly respected in our community. He is good to our people close by and to others far away. And most importantly, he is good to you and me, his family. I'm very grateful for him."

Elisabeth was glad for the opportunity to teach Hurit and her mother how to knit. While she didn't have as much wool as she would have liked, she had enough for each of them to knit a scarf. While Hurit was knitting her scarf, Wawestseka worked with Elisabeth to prepare a buckskin dress and moccasins. The leather parts were cut from tanned hides with a knife and then sewn together with untanned rawhide. They took the time to decorate the top part of the dress with porcupine quills. Elisabeth was thrilled with the results! When she tried it on, Wawestseka exclaimed, "The dress is beautiful on you!" And Hurit added, "Now we look like sisters."

Elisabeth could not help but wonder what Rembrandt might say if he saw her in the buckskin dress. How different it was from the red dress his sister had her try on at the van Rijn home in Leiden. She retrieved her gratefulness journal and looked through it until she found Rembrandt's sketch of her wearing the dress and the hat.

"My friend across the ocean drew this picture of me," Elisabeth told Hurit and her mother. They both gasped at the detailed drawing, and at how much the picture looked like Elisabeth. Elisabeth needed Samoset's help in telling them about her friend, Rembrandt, and about his dream to someday paint beautiful pictures.

Emotion overcame Elisabeth as she recalled her friendship with Rembrandt. She would never forget the closeness she felt to him when they said goodbye to one another in Leiden. Those thoughts prompted memories of her dear parents. Less than a year had passed since she had been in Leiden, and even less time since her aunt, uncle, and parents had died. In a way, it seemed like such a long time ago. Part of her wished she could go back to what used to be normal.

Wawestseka recognized Elisabeth's surge of emotion and put her arms around her. The closeness brought an outpouring of emotion for Elisabeth, but it was beneficial therapy. Wawestseka continued to hold Elisabeth until her crying stopped. After a long sigh, Elisabeth looked up at Wawestseka. "Thank you," she said with a smile. The cry was a good release for Elisabeth. The closeness to Hurit's mother and the genuine friendship she felt from the family helped her feel good about where she was. She was grateful to be alive, to have friends like Hurit and her mother, and to be on an adventure that she could never have imagined. "Thank you," she said again to Wawestseka. "I'm so glad I met Hurit, and that she brought me here."

The three full moons with Hurit and her family came to an end more quickly than Elisabeth thought possible. During her time there, Elisabeth and Hurit both turned 14 years old. A few nights before she was to leave Hurit's home to return to Plymouth, Elisabeth sat by the fire with her new family. In a reflective mood, she took out her gratefulness journal and wrote the following poem:

> I crossed the ocean
> Lived through the cold
> Supported by friends
> I felt the sun.
>
> It began with a dream
> Followed by tears
> I found new friends
> We felt the sun.
>
> Relationships shared
> Friends became family
> Sorrow turned to joy
> We walked in the sun
>
> Faint-hearted to begin
> Buoyed through storm
> Sustained by love
> I experienced the sun.

The time came for Samoset to return to Sowams to meet with Massasoit and his advisors. Elisabeth was grateful that Hurit would again accompany her father on the journey. At their departure, the emotional good-bye to Wawestseka caught Elisabeth by surprise. She knew she had grown close to Hurit's mother but did not realize Wawestseka cared so deeply for her. Their parting hugs were tearful. Neither knew when they might meet again. Missy, sensing the emotion, pressed against Elisabeth's leg.

Chapter 42. Homecoming

Elisabeth saw the girls before they saw her. She and Hurit and Samoset had come out from the tree line at Plymouth. Desire and Mary were on the edge of a field of ripe barley, just north and west of the buildings. Samoset and Hurit stopped as Elisabeth ran toward the girls with Missy leading the way. The girls looked up, startled. They recognized Missy but saw what at first looked like a Native American girl running toward them. Elisabeth called their names. Desire and Mary could hardly believe what they were seeing. Could this possibly be Elisabeth? Finally, Desire recognized the smile and long, light brown hair, and knew it was Elisabeth. "It's Elisabeth!" she shouted and ran toward her. Mary followed close behind. The girls hugged, stepped back to look at one another, and tears of joy flowed.

"It really is you!" said Mary.

"I thought you were a Native American girl," said Desire. "Welcome home! We missed you so much! And look at you! I just love your buckskin dress...and your moccasins! And the sun has browned your skin – and given you freckles! They look good on you!"

Elisabeth turned and motioned for Hurit and Samoset to come. They and Missy all walked together past the barley field, tall corn, and to the head of Plymouth's 'main street,' now called Leiden Street. Governor Bradford was glad – and relieved – to see Elisabeth back as was every other resident of Plymouth. Perhaps it was the buckskin dress, or just the being away for the summer, but Elisabeth looked more grown-up. It was not hard to tell that the three months away had been good for her.

That evening Elisabeth sat around a community fire with Desire, Mary, Priscilla, and Constance. She learned that while she was away, Francis Eaton and Dorothy Jones had been married. They took a cue from Edward Winslow and Susanna White. Francis' wife, Sarah, died leaving him alone with 1-year old Samuel. He asked for Dorothy's hand in marriage, and she gladly accepted. Elisabeth could see how happy Dorothy was, and felt so happy for her. She also was relieved to learn that no one else had died – such a reprieve from all the losses during the terrible winter.

She heard Governor Bradford tell Samoset about the bountiful crops of corn, squash, beans, and barley that had grown over the summer. "We've just begun to gather in our crops," said Bradford, "and there is much more we will bring in. Our first days here in Plymouth were very trying. Now there is much for which we can rejoice! Squanto showed us how to plant corn and fertilize with fish – and it is you, Samoset, who brought Squanto to us. We are very grateful."

"I am glad we both chose the path of peace and not war," said Samoset. It's good to see your crops are plentiful." Samoset reflected for a few moments, then continued, "In the past, our experience with the English and the French has been very mixed. Before we met you, we considered attacking your settlement and ridding you from our land. Massasoit showed great patience and restraint in coming to talk with you. Some advisors counseled him to kill all of you rather than negotiate a peace treaty. His hope continues to be that peace will strengthen our people as well as you."

"When you go to Massasoit, tell him we are grateful to be at peace with him. Tell him we would like him to come to visit with us at the next full moon," said Governor Bradford. "Most of our corn and other crops will be harvested by that time. We can rejoice together for our good crops and our peaceful relationship."

Elisabeth nudged Hurit and spoke to her in the Abenaki language, "I am glad you will be coming back soon for a visit. I'll miss you while you're gone." Elisabeth knew she had found a lifelong friend in Hurit. The two girls hugged.

Squanto nudged Samoset, and said, "Do you remember at Hurit's birth when you gave your daughter to me to hold? I asked the Great Spirit that she would form strong friendships and be a good communicator like you. See? It is happening here right before our eyes!"

Some nearby heard Elisabeth communicate with Hurit in Abenaki. Squanto and Samoset smiled because they understood what Elisabeth said. Others, including Desire, Mary, Priscilla, Constance, Governor Bradford, and John Howland, were amazed at the ease with which Elisabeth seemed to speak to Hurit in Abenaki, now Elisabeth's third language.

Hurit and Samoset stayed overnight before heading the next morning to Sowams.

Chapter 43. Rejoicing for a Bountiful Harvest

Before the first of September, the men began harvesting barley. First, they cut it with a scythe, then tied it in bundles, and stooked it for drying. It was labor-intensive, but the whole community was looking forward to using the new crop to brew a new supply of beer. While the spring water nearby was fresh, clean, and plentiful, all had grown up drinking beer, and they missed not having it. The supply of beer brought from the Mayflower was exhausted. A new batch would be welcomed.

During September, Elisabeth and friends and others in the community picked corn and beans and squash as they became ready. The corn was dried for storage over the coming winter. Corn that was not dried could be used for a short time, but without being dried, it would soon mold and rot.

During that first harvest season, residents of Plymouth noticed changes beginning in the leaves of the surrounding forest. They had never seen such beautiful colors. In England and Holland, leaves just went from green to yellow or brown in the fall, but here the colors were becoming a riot of reds, orange, yellow, purple, and virtually every shade in between.

One day while picking corn, Elisabeth told her friends the story Samoset had related about the legend of the red cob of corn. She recalled the story because Priscilla Mullins had just found an ear of red corn. After hearing the story, Priscilla laughed and said, "I'm going to put this cob of corn where John Alden can find it," – then she blushed, but continued, "and I hope someone tells John what a red cob of corn means!" The girls already knew that Priscilla Mullins and John Alden were attracted to one another. Maybe if John heard the story, it would do for John what it had done for Samoset, prompting him to publicly declare his love.

Elisabeth didn't realize an opportunity to tell John Alden the story about a red cob of corn would present itself so soon. She and Desire were sitting together by the fire that very evening. Priscilla had gone with Mary Chilton to check on Susanna (White) Winslow's baby, Peregrine. John came to add wood to the fire. Desire spoke up and said, "John, Elisabeth has a story to tell you." He smiled at the girls, finished tending the fire, and came to sit with them. "Okay," he said. "I'm ready for a good story."

Elisabeth felt a bit shy about telling John the story, but the shyness didn't hold her back. John laughed heartily when she finished, and then said, "I could have used one of those ears of red corn when I first saw Priscilla on the Mayflower," he chuckled. "Don't tell Priscilla, but I'm going to look through those corn plants tomorrow until I find a red cob!" With that, he got up and walked over to sit beside John Howland. Soon the two of them were laughing together – no doubt about the 'cob of red corn' story. "I hope John finds a red cob for Priscilla," said Desire. "Me too," responded Elisabeth. "Maybe he will start a new tradition here."

True to his word, John Alden searched corn plants the next day for a cob of red corn. When the girls heard a "Whoopy!" from him, they knew he found one. His shout drew the attention of several men as well as the girls, and a group of people came to find out what was happening. John was already in search of Priscilla. He knew she couldn't be far away, and indeed she wasn't. With William Brewster and Governor Bradford looking on, he said, "Priscilla Mullins, I learned last night about a Native American tradition that says finding a red cob of corn means I can ask a girl for a kiss. May I kiss you?" Priscilla's response was hardly shy. "I'm glad you heard the story, John, and yes, you may!"

Every onlooker had a huge smile on his or her face. The girls were particularly happy for Priscilla! A week later, just before the full moon in September, John Alden and Priscilla Mullins asked Governor Bradford to marry them.

Elisabeth thought the timing was perfect. Hurit and her father arrived the day before the wedding and were able to witness an English wedding. They had come to let Governor Bradford know that Massasoit and most of his village would arrive in three days to celebrate with the English for the bountiful harvest they had heard about and for the peace that existed between the two groups.

The Priscilla Mullins-John Alden wedding ceremony was simple. Elisabeth, Hurit, and the other teen girls picked wildflowers. Some became Priscilla's bouquet, and others the girls wove into a tiara for Priscilla to wear on her head. She and Governor Bradford walked side by side down a space between people seated on the ground. The two walked slowly, in step with a drummer who played rhythmically off to one side. In front of the seated group John Alden waited. When Governor Bradford and Priscilla arrived where John was standing, John took Priscilla's hand. Governor Bradford turned to face the couple. He asked, "Do you pledge commitment and faithfulness to one another?" John responded, "Yes, I do," then Priscilla answered similarly.

Governor Bradford stated, "By the authority granted to me by God and this company, I pronounce you to be husband and wife." He talked briefly about their responsibility to one another, and the community's obligation to support and encourage their relationship. The whole of the town witnessed the ceremony, which took only about fifteen minutes. Then they all brought together food they had prepared and enjoyed dinner around a communal fire. A new supply of beer from the recently harvested barley crop was not yet ready. However, Governor Bradford declared that enough brandy or 'strong water' remained for men, women, and children to all have a taste.

The rather impromptu wedding celebration turned out to be a dress rehearsal for a much larger party a few days later. Massasoit arrived with over 100 people from his village, including men, women, and children. They brought with them five freshly killed deer. The English supplied ducks, fish, oysters, wild turkeys, and fresh corn. Preparations were a sight to behold. Virtually every individual was involved in one way or another. Wood spits were constructed to roast the deer and birds; firewood was gathered and brought to spits and to other fires used for cooking pots and roasting of fish; spits needed to be turned. It was mid-afternoon by the time the food was ready. There were not enough clay plates for everyone, and the English had no forks or spoons. Knives were used to cut meat from the roasts. Most people used bark for holding their meat, corn, and seafood. Others simply used their hands.

While no one mentioned it in conversation, Elisabeth noticed that Native Americans outnumbered the English by more than 2 to 1. It didn't seem to matter to individuals or to either group regarding enjoyment or engagement. Everyone shared in preparations, cooking, eating, and mingling. Socializing was easier for Elisabeth because she understood much of what the Pokanokets said. She noticed that many of their words and expressions were the same as the Abenaki language she was learning, and with a few questions of her own, she was able to understand what was said and explain it to her girlfriends. On a few occasions, she even interpreted for some of the men.

It would have been hard for Elisabeth to pick one favorite part of the celebration: no one could have done without the amazing and plentiful food; camaraderie during preparation, eating, and clean-up was pleasurable; and the dancing after the meal was so much fun.

The dancing began with four of Massasoit's men setting up drums in a semi-circle. The rhythm was such that most people who heard it couldn't help but want to move their feet. First, the Native American men began to dance around the drummers. Before long, Hurit had organized the teen girls and boys to form their own dance circle. Pretty much all the English young people were a bit awkward at the start, but Hurit was able to say in English, "Watch my feet and follow me." They did, and with a bit of stumbling and a lot of laughing, ten English teens – Elisabeth, Desire, Mary, Constance, and six teenage boys who had survived the winter - participated in the dance circle with Native American teens.

Governor Bradford was with William Brewster and his wife, Mary, watching the dancing. "What do you think, Mr. Brewster?" he asked. Is this dancing uplifting for our children?" Mrs. Brewster jumped in to respond before her husband had time to answer. "Look at them laughing and having such a good time!" she said. "I think it is wonderfully therapeutic for them."

"Yes," agreed her husband, "perhaps they need this kind of play. Laughter is good medicine for young and old!"

Mr. Brewster reflected for a moment, and then said, "When it comes to these kinds of questions – questions about whether certain activities are appropriate - I often ask myself, 'What would Pastor Robinson say if he were here?' And I can hear him asking, 'Is it honest, pure, lovely, and good?' What I see in the dance circles certainly meets those conditions."

"Besides," Mr. Brewster continued, "Pastor Robinson said that an important part of our task in America would be to build charitable relationships with Natives. I think we are accomplishing that here today."

Meanwhile, so much food was prepared for the harvest and friendship festivities that it carried on into a second day and part of a third. It was like a family celebration in which everyone was having such a good time, no one really wanted to leave. Friendships - cordial, cross-cultural friendships - were built among the teens and among younger children. How different history would be if such relationships had been the norm!

After a mid-day meal on the third day, Massasoit and his band said their good-byes and soon disappeared into the forest.

Chapter 44. The Fortune

In November of 1621, the Nausets on Cape Cod saw a ship arrive off their coast. Within a few days, word spread through the Native American underground until it came to Massasoit in Sowams, and finally to Squanto and the English in Plymouth. No one knew the nationality of the ship, and Governor Bradford was concerned it might be a French ship coming to attack Plymouth. He directed Miles Standish, "Make preparations to defend our settlement."

The ship came slowly toward Plymouth harbor. Before it dropped anchor, Mr. Standish recognized it as an English ship. His announcement brought much joy to the community. The ship turned out to be the Fortune. It arrived from England with 31 single men aboard and four married couples.

However, joy for the Plymouth community did not last long. The passengers on the Fortune brought no new supplies of food, and little in the way of extra clothing or bedding. It meant that there were an additional 39 people to feed over the coming winter, and housing would not be easy. Most of the men bunked in the four community shelters that had been built in addition to seven family houses.

"Make a list of all our food supplies," Governor Bradford directed. What he learned from the inventory told a grim picture. He reported to an assembly of the settlers, "Based on our current stores, we have a food crisis in our community that will extend through the winter. Rations for everyone will be cut by one half. By doing that, I estimate that our supplies will last through late spring – about five months from now." The portions of food allocated for each person meant that the community survived, but hunger was a constant companion throughout the remainder of the winter for all residents.

During the Fortune's unloading process, Desire learned that the ship would be returning to England in two weeks. That same night she talked with Elisabeth until the wee hours of the morning. Desire felt strongly about her need to return to Leiden to be with her mother. "I miss my mom terribly," she said, "and if I don't try to see her now, I may never see her again. I see what you and Mary and Priscilla have lost," she continued. "You had no choice about losing your parents. By going back, I may have the opportunity to see at least part of my family again."

"Oh, Desire!" said Elisabeth, "I'll miss you so much!"

"And I will miss you and Mary, and Priscilla, and Constance, and Dorothy," responded Desire. Through the darkness she looked intently at Elisabeth. "You, my dear friend, are especially made for this new land. Already you speak a Native American language. You've made a Native American friend; you wear a buckskin dress and moccasins. You seem to be in harmony with all that is here; and this beautiful, wild land, and people are in harmony with you. I know your life here will be fulfilling. Your destiny is in this new land, Elisabeth; mine is not."

"Desire, I would love for you to stay," said Elisabeth, "but even more, I want what is best for you. If you must go, you have my full support. But know that I'll never forget you." Elisabeth paused, then said with a smile, "If I ever have a daughter, her name will be Desire. I want her to be just like you! You have been such a faithful friend." Elisabeth felt a mixture of joy and sadness. Saying good-bye to Desire brought back the memory of saying farewell to Rembrandt.

The two girls hugged and cried and fell asleep, wondering what their different futures might bring. In the morning, they talked with Governor Bradford to tell him of Desire's wish to return to her mother.

In consultation with William Brewster, he agreed that the move back to Leiden to be with her mother would be in Desire's best interests.

Early on the morning of December 13, 1621, Desire boarded a shallop that would take her out to the Fortune. Elisabeth was there for one final hug, then watched as the shallop sailed to the Fortune where Desire boarded the larger ship. Tears blurred her vision as the sails on the Fortune were raised, and the ship – and Desire – began their return voyage across the ocean.

The two girls would not meet again, but Elisabeth's first-born child was a girl. Elisabeth named her Desire.

Chapter 45. Two Red Cobs

The Spring of 1622 saw the planting of crops continue as Squanto had shown the previous year. A herring was embedded in the earth with each kernel of corn.

Most of the residents of Plymouth worked together in a communal effort. However, John Howland approached Governor Bradford with the idea of individual families looking after their own plot of land for planting and maintaining crops. John had noticed that not all who worked at planting were equally ambitious, nor did they seem to tend the crops with the care he thought was needed. Yet the harvest was divided evenly throughout the community.

Governor Bradford agreed that John could go ahead if he could get at least two other families to participate in the experiment. William Brewster and Edward Winslow both liked John's idea and agreed to join in having their individual families plant crops. Each family was allotted one acre of land to work. At harvest time, they would be able to keep whatever they had grown and tended.

As it turned out, the experiment was an unqualified success for the three families – so much so that the following year, Governor Bradford mandated that all the corn planting was to be done by individual family groups.

The experiment had some unintended outcomes. Or, as some thought in looking back, maybe the unintended results were, indeed, intended. It brought the three families together more often in a social setting. They shared the camaraderie of self-reliance, and it allowed the opportunity to talk about what worked well on their own acre of land,

and what did not. And it meant that two young men, John Howland and John Winslow, Edward's younger brother who had arrived on the Fortune, spent time interacting with Elisabeth Tilley and Mary Chilton. Both girls turned 15 years old during the summer of 1622.

In late August, Hurit and her father, Samoset, stopped in Plymouth as they had the previous year. Samoset was on his way to Sowams to meet with Massasoit and his advisory group of Sachems. Normally, Samoset would not have stopped at Plymouth, but he knew Hurit was anxious to see Elisabeth. Besides, Wawestseka had made a new set of moccasins for Elisabeth. "The ones we made for her when she was here must be worn out by now," she had said.

"We will stay one night at Plymouth, and then we must go to Sowams," Samoset told Hurit.

The girls enjoyed the evening in Plymouth, sitting and chatting together by the community fire. They spoke at times in English and at times in Abenaki. Elisabeth told Hurit about Desire's leaving to go back to her mother in Leiden. Hurit, of course, delivered the moccasins her mother had made for Elisabeth. "She missed you not being with us this summer," Hurit told Elisabeth, "and it gave her great pleasure to make these for you."

Elisabeth told Hurit about the experiment she was involved with in growing corn. In doing so, she indicated to Hurit who John Howland was on the other side of the fire. "He is the person who suggested we try it," she said. He has been so thoughtful of me in the work we do together. Sometimes I've wanted to give him a big hug – but I haven't yet."

Perhaps intuitively knowing the girls were talking about him, John Howland came and sat near them. "I wish I could understand what you two Native Americans are talking about," he said with a smile.

"I will consider that a compliment, John Howland," said Elisabeth. "You just wish you could have buckskin clothing so you can look like us."

John had a good belly laugh. "Yes, buckskin clothes would probably be more comfortable than my wool breaches," he said, "but I think I'd need pants rather than a dress."

"Hurit," Elisabeth said, "this man, John Howland, is a miracle man. He really shouldn't be here with us. During a bad storm on our voyage, a huge wave washed him overboard in the middle of the ocean."

Hurit looked at both John and Elisabeth and asked, "How did you ever get back on the ship?"

"Tell her the story, John," said Elisabeth.

After John recounted his harrowing experience, Hurit said, "I'm glad you survived so you are here now, John."

Elisabeth turned to John and asked, "Are you serious about wanting to wear buckskin clothes?"

"Of course, I'm serious," replied John.

"Well, maybe, just maybe…if you bring me enough deer skin, I will help you make buckskin clothes. Hurit and her parents taught me well. You're the first person in Plymouth to say they would like to wear buckskin clothes like ours."

"Ok, but remember I need pants and a jacket," said John. "I would not look good in a dress." And the three had a good laugh together.

"I'll keep that in mind," said Elisabeth. "Now Hurit and I are going to our beds for the night. She must leave early tomorrow with her father, and I'll be up with her to say goodbye. Besides, our corn is ready for harvest, so I will get to the cornfield before the day gets too warm."

"Good-night to you both," said John. "See you in the morning." As he walked toward his own home, he couldn't help but think to himself, "I know what I'm going to do when I find a cob of red corn!"

The next morning, Elisabeth was up early to see Hurit and her father off. The two girls both recognized their deepening connection with one another. Each time they met, it seemed their bond grew stronger. "I can hardly wait until you come for a visit again, Hurit. I'm grateful for your friendship." After a warm hug, the girls went their separate ways.

It took a few days, but much to his delight, John Howland found a cob of red corn. The first thing he did was slip over to the Winslow's field to tell John Winslow what he had discovered – and what it meant. John had a good laugh and asked John Howland who he was going to ask for a kiss. "Elisabeth Tilley, of course," Howland responded. "She has such a great sense of humor, and I love how she looks in those buckskin clothes. I've watched how hard she's worked on the crops this summer. I think she's a perfect fit for this new land – and," he added a bit self-consciously, "for me."

"No doubt she's a good one," said John Winslow. "I have my eye on Mary Chilton. Her smile just about makes me melt, she's soooo good with Susanna's kids - and I know she would be good for me."

"Well, you better keep an eye out for your own red cob of corn, brother," laughed John Howland. "I know Elisabeth knows what this red cob of corn means, so I'm going to find her. I hope she says, yes!"

John Winslow didn't exactly follow John Howland as Howland went to find Elisabeth, but he was close enough to them to hear what was said when they met. "Look what I found," John said to Elisabeth. Elisabeth smiled, blushed a little, and said, "And what do you plan to do now that you found a red cob of corn, John Howland?"

John didn't hesitate. Looking intently into her eyes, he said, "I'm here to ask you for a kiss, Elisabeth." She didn't drop her gaze. Her brief pause felt like an eternity to John as she looked deeply into his eyes. At last, he heard, "Yes, John. I'm glad you asked..."

Listening but out of sight, John Winslow smiled and said to himself, "I hope Mary Chilton says the same thing!" Before the end of the week, John Winslow had indeed found his own cob of red corn and approached Mary. Mary Chilton had pretty much the same response.

Chapter 46. Déjà Vu

Elisabeth was picking corn near the end of a row when she looked up to see Hurit coming towards her out of the tree line. She had not expected to see Hurit again until the full moon in September, so it was a pleasant surprise – and at first, concerning to Elisabeth when Hurit arrived alone at the first quarter of the moon. She alerted Mrs. Brewster that Hurit had come and that they would take some time to talk.

The day was hot, and the two girls went for a walk by the ocean. "Ok, Hurit. I know something important has happened. I hope it's good news!"

Hurit's excitement was palpable. "Elisabeth, I'm going to get married!" Before Elisabeth could ask any questions, Hurit's story spilled out, "One evening, about a week after my father and I arrived in Sowams, we were in our beds after sunset. Just before it was fully dark, we heard the music of a flute from outside our wetu. "What is that music?" I asked my father.

"It sounds like a courting flute," he told me. "The Pokanokets have a custom whereby young men court the girl they want to marry by playing the courting flute near the girl's wetu." Then my father asked, "Is there a young man here who you think is interested in you?"

I was quiet for a moment, then I said to him, "Yes, Ahanu, the runner who has carried messages to you at our home in the north has been very attentive to me each time you and I come here."

I was so surprised when my father said, "I'm not surprised that it is Ahanu. I have noticed his attention to you. You can ignore the courting flute if you do not care for him. If he is the person you want to be your husband, then when you are ready, you can thank him for playing the flute for you. If you do that, Ahanu will know you are open to his courting, and he will talk with his father and with me about marriage. Then his father will talk to the rest of his family to learn if they are in favor of his marriage to you."

Hurit continued her story, "I felt overwhelmed that night at the prospect of such a profound change in my life. And marrying a man from a village so far from my own home would be another huge change. Most girls in my village marry a man from our local community – or at least some place that's closer than Sowams. So, I listened to Ahanu play beautifully on the flute. So many thoughts went through my mind I had a hard time sleeping. In the morning, I asked my father if he thought Ahanu would be a good man for me. My father said, "Ahanu is trustworthy. Massasoit sends messages with him to all the Sachems. I have also seen that Ahanu is kind and considerate of others. But it is vital to listen carefully to your own heart. Your heart will be at peace if Ahanu is right for you in every way."

"Thank you, father," I said. And then I almost surprised myself by asking, "Would it be ok with you if I went to Patuxet – to Plymouth – to talk with Elisabeth?" I told him that he and I had done that walk many times, and I was sure of the way. My father thought for a few moments and then said, "Yes. That would be good. I am meeting with Massasoit and others for several days. Just be sure to return here before seven days have passed."

So, here I am, Elisabeth. I've thought a lot about Ahanu on my way here. I just needed someone to talk to."

Is he much older than you are?" asked Elisabeth.

"He is about five years older – maybe a bit more, but he is strong and handsome, and I know he is trustworthy – or Massasoit would not have him as a runner. And," Hurit added with a smile, "he plays the flute very well!"

"I hear very clearly what your heart is saying," said Elisabeth with a smile. "Tell me what you think."

"My heart wants to be with him because it sees what a wonderful person he is, Elisabeth," said Hurit, "but my heart also tugs at leaving my family and my village."

Elisabeth was quiet for a few moments, then said, "The distance from your family and your village may not seem as great when you are with someone who really cares for you, Hurit, and the distance to Ahanu's home in Sowams might seem awfully great if you choose your family over Ahanu."

The girls sat together on a rock. "I'm so glad I came to talk with you, Elisabeth. My decision seems quite simple now. I will go back to Sowams, and when Ahanu plays his flute again, I will let him know his courting is welcome."

The two girls looked at one another. "I'm so happy for you," said Elisabeth. "Now, do I have a story for you!" Hurit listened as Elisabeth told the story of John Howland finding the cob of red corn. "Did he ask you about marriage?" Hurit asked.

"Not yet, but I think that conversation may be coming soon," replied Elisabeth with a smile.

Chapter 47. Planning

At the full moon, Hurit and her father returned to Plymouth. On this visit, Hurit had a beautiful bearskin robe with her. It was already evening, and Elisabeth brought Hurit to sit near the fire. The two joined Mary Chilton, John Winslow, and John Howland.

"The bearskin is absolutely beautiful, Hurit!" Mary exclaimed. "Please tell us about it."

"As you know, I am from the Abenaki tribe in Pemaquid. The man who is courting me, Ahanu, is a Pokanoket from Sowams. The gift of a bearskin is a public way to tell our communities that he is courting me. By giving me the bearskin, Ahanu is telling his family and community about his intention to marry me, and that his father approves. If anyone in Ahanu's community disapproves, they can talk with Ahanu's father to say why they disapprove. When I wear the bearskin robe at my home, my people will know that I am being courted. If they disapprove, they can talk with my father."

"If everyone approves, when will you get married," asked Elisabeth.

"We will marry in the spring," said Hurit. "Ahanu and I both think spring is a good time for new things to start."

Hurit looked inquiringly at Elisabeth. She wanted to ask whether she and John Howland had talked about marriage, but was hesitant to do so while John was sitting there. The question she asked was, "What news do you have, Elisabeth?"

Elisabeth looked over at John. Their eyes met, and she read his approval to tell about their plans.

"John asked me to be his wife," said Elisabeth, "and I was delighted to say 'Yes.' "We haven't set a time to marry." John was close enough to reach over and hold Elisabeth's hand.

Elisabeth looked over at Mary and said, "Mary, now it's your turn to share news with Hurit."

Tears of joy came to Mary's eyes. "After the sadness and hardships we experienced when we first came here, it's hard to believe there could be so much happiness in one place!" she said. "John Winslow asked me to be his wife, and I was thrilled when he did." She reached out to hold John's hand. "We haven't yet set a time to get married, either."

The group sat quietly for a few minutes, each seemingly lost in thought. John Howland spoke up, "It really is a miracle that any of us are sitting here tonight. Yet despite a raging sea, sickness, cold, different cultures, and different languages, here we are. We could all just as easily be dead – and none of us could have imagined meeting Hurit." He paused for a moment as an idea continued to form in his mind. He squeezed Elisabeth's hand and continued, "Here's an idea we can all think about. What if we were all to get married at the same time on the same day in the same place?"

Hurit looked at Elisabeth and Mary, and then at the two Johns. She saw what appeared to be shock on their faces and then smiles start to form. The smiles transitioned to joyous laughter - laughter that brought tears to each of their eyes. "What a great idea!" exclaimed Elisabeth.

Governor Bradford, Hurit's father Samoset, the Brewsters, and the Winslows were on the other side of the fire and could not help but overhear the laughter from the group of young people. "Oh, it's so good to hear and see laughter like that!" exclaimed Governor Bradford.

"Yes," responded Mary Brewster. "I wondered at times if we would ever hear laughter here in Plymouth. It makes my heart sing!"

Samoset had just finished telling the Governor and others in the group about his daughter's upcoming marriage to Ahanu.

"You are not the only one to have a wedding going on," added Edward Winslow. "My brother is quite smitten with Mary Chilton, and John Howland with Elisabeth Tilley. Governor Bradford will soon need to officiate at a couple of weddings here in Plymouth."

Back on the other side of the fire, Hurit, said, "I think Plymouth would be an ideal place for a triple wedding. Ahanu and I would not have to worry about choosing between his village or my village for a wedding location. And besides, my mother has often said she would like to see where Elisabeth lives. I think she would be glad to see our wedding here."

"You mentioned Spring, Hurit, as the time you and Ahanu were planning a wedding," said Elisabeth.

"Yes, Ahanu and I are both determined to have a Spring wedding when the first warm weather comes after the winter. It is time for new beginnings, and in future years, springtime will remind us of when we started our life together – and of the importance of renewal. It also allows me to go home to Pemaquid Point, talk with my mother. She will want to be a part of our wedding planning."

"I like the idea of a spring wedding and connection to revitalization," said Mary. "My parents were married many years, and I remember my mother saying how important it was for them both to reaffirm their commitment to one another through the years – kind of like a renewal."

"I really like the idea of the three of us getting married – same day, same place, same time," said Elisabeth. "Each of us has some work to do if we are going to make it happen. Your parents and Ahanu's parents will need to agree, Hurit – and would you need Massasoit's approval?"

"No," responded Hurit. "Our families decide on where and when a wedding should happen. And we really don't have a right and wrong way to do a wedding ceremony. Parents talk about what they think should happen. Elders do not need to give approval."

"Mary," continued Elisabeth, "you and I will need to get approval from Governor Bradford – for our own marriages, and make sure he will include Hurit and Ahanu in a ceremony. And it would be proper for me to also ask permission of the Brewsters since I am living with them."

"I can't wait to talk with Susanna about a triple wedding," said Mary. "I already told her that John asked me to be his wife, and she is so happy for us. I know she will be very supportive of whatever we decide to do. And if anyone needs any convincing, Susanna certainly knows how to do that. In fact," said Mary, "Susanna is so persuasive I know she will get Governor Bradford and the Brewsters onboard if they have any reservations."

And so it was that three young, 15-year old brides-to-be – mature beyond their years – began planning a day they would remember for the rest of their lives. The two Johns knew they were in for quite a ride. Though Ahanu did not yet know what was coming, Hurit felt sure he would be pleased with the plan.

"Weddings here are pretty simple," said John Howland. "Not much ceremony. Tell us about Native American weddings, Hurit," he continued. "What traditions do you have that we could incorporate?"

"Our weddings include a community feast and then dancing – not very different from the celebration we had here last year to celebrate your harvest," said Hurit.

"I heard that was quite a party," said John Winslow.

"It was!" responded Mary. "We had so much fun, especially dancing."

"Do you have any specific wedding traditions that we might not know about?" Elisabeth asked Hurit.

"You might not know about the pipe ceremony," responded Hurit. It's the most solemn part of our weddings. Each set of parents of the couple getting married brings a pipe and tobacco. It's all very symbolic. Families, friends, and elders share the smoking of the pipes in a circle. It is a way to show that the community is coming together to support the couple."

"Do the couples getting married smoke the pipe, too?" asked John Howland.

"Oh, yes," replied Hurit. "That is essential. They are the reason others are coming together in support."

"Hmmm," mused John Winslow. "If pipe smoking is part of the weddings, I hope my brother, Edward, and Governor Bradford and William Brewster will participate."

"Mrs. Brewster is quite open-minded, and she may be a good ally if we need to convince others," said Elisabeth. "She told me last year that she and her husband intervened with Governor Bradford when he had reservations about our dancing at the harvest celebration."

"And what are you young people talking about so earnestly?" asked Mr. Brewster. He, Governor Bradford, Susanna Winslow, and Samoset had just come over from the other side of the campfire. The young people were so engrossed in their discussion, they had not seen the others approach.

"We're talking about spring weddings," said John Howland, "and we have some intriguing questions to ask. But it's far better that I let the girls tell you what they are thinking of."

Elisabeth, Mary, and Hurit each talked about their desire for a triple wedding. Governor Bradford had no problem in marrying the three girls. "As you know, we believe weddings should be a civil affair," he said. "The Bible does not give us any examples of church weddings. Samoset, what are your thoughts about Hurit getting married here at Plymouth?"

Samoset smiled and said, "I think it would be fine. But that man is a sage," he said, pointing to John Howland. "He knows the importance of deferring to a woman for planning. It is much more important for my wife to be part of that kind of preparation than for me. It must work for her, or it will not be a good idea. If my wife and Ahanu's parents are ok with our children being married at Plymouth, I am happy to see her marriage take place here with new friends."

"There are Native American customs important to Hurit and her family - such as the pipe circle we would like to include," said Elisabeth to Governor Brewer. "Would you consider joining us for a custom like that?"

"We have not yet done the pipe circle here at Plymouth, though Governor Carver smoked a pipe with Massasoit when they first negotiated a peace agreement," the Governor responded. After a pause, he continued, "Your brother, Edward," Bradford said to John Winslow, "and Stephen Hopkins smoked a pipe with Massasoit when they went to visit him in Sowams last year."

Turning to Samoset, Governor Bradford continued, "Tell us about the symbolism of smoking a pipe and the pipe circle."

Samoset responded, "Smoking of the pipe sometimes just means a celebration of friendship. Sometimes it represents a covenant or agreement. That is what it means at the weddings of our sons and daughters. Our families and friends will form a pipe circle to show support of their promise to live together. Those joining the circle are saying they will encourage the couple when difficult times come."

"Well," mused Governor Bradford, "the pipe circle certainly sounds appropriate. You have my approval for that."

"Thank you, Governor Bradford," said Mary. "I know there will be other Native American customs at the wedding. You saw the dancing at our celebration of harvest last year. That was such a happy occasion, and Hurit says we will see the drummers and dancing again at the weddings."

"Well, I wondered about the dancing last year," Governor Bradford responded. "It is so different from our English customs." Motioning to William Brewster, he continued, "Both Mr. and Mrs. Brewster noticed the laughter and good time that the dancing brought to you young people – and older folks as well. I see no reason it should not be part of special times of celebration with our Native friends."

"Oh, Governor Bradford," said Elisabeth, "Celebrating together will be so meaningful – and so much fun. Thank you."

"You are the future of our settlement," responded Governor Bradford. "I hope the connections you are making with Hurit and her family will be embraced by others in our community."

"I am so excited," said Mary, "our weddings will be nothing like I ever imagined!"

"Perhaps," said Samoset, "our daughters' weddings will lead to increased trust between our cultures."

"That would indeed be a welcome outcome," replied Governor Bradford.

And then there were lots of hugs before the group separated for the night.

Sadly, an increase in trust was not the eventual outcome in the relationship between the English and Native Americans. Despite a positive start, issues of greed, power, control, and mistrust eventually led to war - and English domination.

Chapter 48. A Difficult Winter

The winter of 1622 was not easy for anyone in Plymouth. Rationing of food was needed again. It was evident to Governor Bradford that communal labor for growing crops did not work well. The only families who had enough food for the winter were the three families who chose to plant and tend their three individual plots of land. The difference was evident to everyone in the community. John Howland, the Brewsters, and the Hopkins' all brought in enough food to more than meet their needs for the winter. Their experiment in planting and tending crops on family acreages worked so well that Governor Bradford decreed all households would be assigned an acre of land on which to grow their own crops in the spring of 1623. If individual families grew and harvested more food than was needed, they could use the extra to trade for other goods or services.

The three families having an abundance of food in storage did, in fact, share with others in the community that winter. However, after an entrepreneurial approach to farming was mandated, no more crop shortages or hungry winters plagued Plymouth in future years. The new system resulted in each member of every household feeling a greater sense of urgency to contribute to the farming process. More purposeful and focused labor occurred in each phase of planting, tending of crops, and harvesting.

In late November of 1622, after Hurit and her father had left Plymouth, Elisabeth experienced another loss. Squanto died while guiding some men from the Plymouth community to a Native American village to the south. There were rumors that Squanto was poisoned by other Native Americans who believed him to be untrustworthy. His relationship with Massasoit had deteriorated. Squanto's actions while in Plymouth confirmed to Massasoit that he was not trustworthy, and Massasoit demanded the English turn Squanto over to face Wampanoag justice. Whether Squanto's death was from a sudden illness or due to a more sinister cause, Elisabeth did not know, but news of his death made her very sad. She had gotten to know Squanto well. He helped her learn Abenaki. He was a catalyst in her friendship with Hurit. She found him to be very intelligent, and thought of him as a friend.

She understood the deep sadness Squanto sometimes felt about his past. On one occasion, he spoke to her about it at length. He told Elisabeth about being violently snatched from his home, returning several years later to find his family and friends dead, and then experiencing the mistrust of other Native Americans. They both recognized that exclusive focus on such events made life seem so unfair. Both knew it was essential to intentionally turn their focus on positive things in their lives – though that was much easier said than done! From time-to-time, some small event in life would trigger a memory.

Elisabeth had undoubtedly experienced many difficult times in her own brief 15 years. She wrote in her gratefulness journal about Squanto's passing, about his friendship to her, and about his support of her friendship with Hurit.

During the coldest months of the winter, the men, and a few of the women of Plymouth built a stockade around the town. Trees were cut from the surrounding forest, branches stripped, and logs hauled to the settlement. Elisabeth thought the wall was unnecessary. From her perspective, Native Americans had been friendly and helpful to the English. Why was a wall needed? However, Governor Bradford knew there were tensions with nearby Native Americans who did not want the English to settle in their land. Past experience told them that continued English presence would not work out well. Massasoit had been clear that not all of his Sachems were in favor of allowing the English to stay. Bradford's military advisor, Miles Standish, warned that the wall was essential for protection, and construction went ahead.

Elisabeth and Mary assisted with the project by helping tamp down the soil around the base of logs placed upright in a trench dug around the perimeter of Plymouth. They used stout sticks about six feet long to tamp the soil. It was tiring work, and by the end of the day, their shoulders and arms ached. But the work kept them active and warm. Some of the men were so weak from lack of food that they collapsed during the building process. The reduced rations were taking a toll. When the stockade was completed, it was nine feet high and extended almost a mile-and-a-half around the perimeter of Plymouth.

Another task that kept Elisabeth busy that winter was making John Howland a pair of buckskin trousers and a buckskin shirt for their upcoming wedding. John had traded an ax to some Pokanokets and received enough deerskin to make several outfits. Elisabeth had sufficient material to make herself a new buckskin jacket and a new set of moccasins in addition to John's attire.

Elisabeth made sure the clothing fit John. She had him try it on, made needed adjustments, and then decorated both of their jackets with porcupine quills and beads given her by Mrs. Brewster. She did not show John the finished clothing until the day before their wedding.

Chapter 49. Hurit Arrives

In mid-March of 1623, spring arrived in Plymouth with exceptionally warm weather. Elisabeth knew Hurit would be on her way to Plymouth soon if she wasn't already. After the completion of the stockade, she and Mary had devoted time to gathering wood suitable for cooking fires. Remembering the harvest celebration in the fall of 1621, the girls knew several fires would be needed for roasting fish, deer, and turkeys, and cooking various stews.

On March 17th, Hurit arrived in Plymouth with her father, mother, three uncles, and their families. Excitement spread through Plymouth. Everyone knew a wedding – actually three weddings – would soon take place. It was a wonderful reunion for Hurit, Elisabeth, and Mary. Elisabeth's first question of Hurit was, "Is Ahanu and his family open to coming here for the wedding?" And she was delighted to hear Hurit's response.

"You know Ahanu is a runner. He came through the heavy snow of winter to visit my family and me in Pemaquid Point. I told him about our idea of getting married in Plymouth, and he agreed it would be a memorable and unique way to start our lives together. His family was at the harvest festival you had two falls ago in Plymouth, and they really enjoyed it – so he assured us that his family would be glad to join us here for the wedding."

"One of my uncles who accompanied us here is a runner. He will travel to Sowams to let Ahanu's family know we are ready for them to come to Plymouth. If it is ok with you, the rest of my family will stay here in Plymouth to prepare for our weddings. Ahanu and his family should be here in four days. So…five days from today will be our big day! Do you think we can be ready?"

"I think we all were ready to get married last fall," said Mary, and the three girls had a hearty laugh.

"Of course, you can stay with us while your uncle goes to Sowams for Ahanu," said Elisabeth.

It was heartening to see how the Plymouth community came together to assist the girls in preparing to host a party for the whole of the Plymouth community and a contingent of Native Americans. Even the somewhat obnoxious Billington boys contributed to preparations by netting a supply of cod and gathering oysters and several dozen enormous lobsters.

Chapter 50. The Supper Before the Weddings

Hurit's uncle, along with Ahanu, his family, and 45 other residents of Sowams, arrived at Plymouth as Hurit had said they would. Massasoit and his family were part of the Sowams contingent. Elisabeth brought John Howland with her to meet Ahanu. She had prepared John to say, "It is my honor to meet you..." in the Abenaki language. While Ahanu's Pokanoket language was slightly different, Elisabeth knew he would understand.

And Ahanu clearly did understand what John said when they met. The big smile lighting his face said it all. Neither Elisabeth or John was prepared for Ahanu's response. Unknown to Elisabeth, Hurit had practiced with Ahanu to greet John in English with almost the exact same words, "It is my honor to meet you, sir." Tears came to Elisabeth's eyes when she saw the handshake between the two young men become an embrace. The two reflected such different cultures: John wearing a cotton shirt, wool pants, and boots, while Ahanu wore only a loincloth. His long black hair and smooth face contrasted with John's light brown hair and reddish beard. They were very nearly the same height. John was a heavier build; Ahanu reflecting the more slender physique of a runner.

Elisabeth, Mary, Hurit and her mother, Wawestseka, Susanna Winslow, and Mary Brewster, worked together organizing and preparing a community dinner. After a challenging winter, the wedding celebration was on, even though the official ceremony would be the next day.

Following the introduction of John to Ahanu, Elisabeth took John to put on his new buckskin clothing. "Here are your wedding clothes, my

Handsome Prince," she said and left him to dress. John came out to Elisabeth, posed with his legs and arms spread, and said, "These are the most beautiful clothes I've ever worn, Elisabeth! How do I look?"

"You are the finest looking man in this New World – and the clothes look good on you, too!" said Elisabeth, laughing. They both had tears in their eyes – partly tears of joy, and perhaps tears that reflected their longing for one another. There was a genuine sense that neither of them should be alive now. John should really have been lost to the sea, and both escaped the sickness from which half of the people who came with them on the Mayflower died. But they were alive – and on the verge of starting life together.

John put his arms around Elisabeth and held her tight. The physical closeness for both was almost overwhelming.

"I'm so glad our wedding is tomorrow," said John. "I need your closeness like I need water and air!"

"Oh, John, I love you so much!" Elisabeth replied. Their hug lingered. Looking up at him, she said, "People are waiting for us. Let's go show off your new clothes."

Chapter 51. Three Weddings and a Party

The wedding ceremonies took place following a late noon meal the next day. Cooking fires were lit in the morning to roast the deer, turkey, and fish. Other fires were dedicated to lobster and oyster preparation.

Each of the three couples was easily distinguishable. Hurit wore a buckskin dress and a beautiful mink shoulder cape. Her black hair was long, tied back, and gleaming with porcupine quills. Ahanu was striking-looking in a moose skin robe. Mary and John Winslow wore their best English clothes: Mary in a blouse and long, flowing skirt; John in dark wool breaches and a light-colored cotton shirt. Elisabeth wore the buckskin dress Hurit's mother had made for her and the buckskin jacket she had made for herself decorated with porcupine quills and beads. John Howland looked very much like he belonged with Elisabeth, wearing the buckskin outfit she had made for him: the fine-looking pants and the shirt she had beautifully decorated.

Governor Bradford officiated for the English part of the weddings. His part of the ceremony was brief, simply asking each couple if they were committed to one another and pronouncing each couple husband and wife based on his authority as Governor of Plymouth Colony. He addressed the crowd, reminding them of their responsibility to support each of the couples through the good times and trying times they would face.

Massasoit took charge of the Native American part of the ceremony. His involvement was not so short. Massasoit was such an impressive looking individual: taller than all the Englishmen and even taller than other Native Americans. His well-developed physique was evident. He wore a red horseman's coat over buckskin pants and sported a copper chain about his neck - gifts given to him by the English prior to the harvest celebration in 1621. He looked every part the proud and confident leader he was. With Samoset's help, Massasoit explained the pipe ceremony.

"The bowl of the pipe is from clay. It represents the earth," he said. "The stem of the pipe is from plants. The whole pipe – bowl and stem – represents connection and unity. The parts of the pipe are joined together to make a whole, just like these couples come together in unity." He continued, "Those who share in the pipe circle choose to be in harmony with the couple being married and say by their participation that they will support the couple in good times and in hard times." Massasoit then invited families and friends of the couples being married to join in the pipe circle.

The wedding couples had not discussed the make-up of the pipe circle. To no one's surprise, Hurit's parents and uncles joined the circle along with other members of Ahanu's family. However, when Elisabeth and John sat together, Elisabeth was delighted that Mrs. Brewster came to sit with her. Mrs. Brewster sat on Elisabeth's left. Mr. Brewster sat to the right of John Howland. Missy would not be left out. She squeezed into the circle and lay between Elisabeth and Mrs. Brewster, seeming to know the importance of being part of the ceremony. John Winslow's brother, Edward, and his wife Susanna joined the circle on either side of Mary and John. Priscilla (Mullins) and husband John Alden formed part of the circle as did Constance Hopkins. The only thing that could have made the moment more perfect for Elisabeth was if her dear friend Desire were there.

Two pipes were shared around the circle: one brought by Hurit's parents, and one brought by Ahanu's parents. Passing of the pipes took considerable time. Occasionally, a pipe needed to be re-stoked or re-lit. Mary Brewster found Elisabeth's hand, which was on Missy's back. She clasped it in her own hand, and whispered to Elisabeth, "It's hard to believe this is really happening! I never imagined myself or my husband ever smoking a pipe – but I'm so glad we're both here with you and John! You're such a perfect couple.1 You were made for one another – and both of you for this New World."

Emotion overflowed for Elisabeth, and she was only able to respond to Mrs. Brewster with a nod. John felt Elisabeth tremble and put his arm around her.

After both pipes made a circuit, Massasoit stood, as did the others in the circle. They all joined hands. Massasoit looked to the sky and spoke a prayer. Elisabeth did not understand the whole of what he said, but she thought it went something like this, "Creator of everything, you know us all. You brought together the couples who are committing to one another today. May their relationship be strong. May their wetu be a place of peace and love."

And then, with a big smile, he said to the group, "And now, when the drummers are ready, we will dance."

Four men formed a semi-circle with their drums and began the beat. Hurit's and Ahanu's families took the lead in creating a dance circle. Soon they were joined by many from Plymouth. Sometimes they formed one large circle, sometimes it was a small circle within a larger circle - as when all three newly married couples were surrounded by a larger circle of family and friends. It was an evening-long remembered by all who attended: two very different cultures interacting, partying, dancing, sharing food. Differences in dress, customs, and language did not matter.

People from both groups, including the newlyweds, drifted in and out of the dance circles. While the drums played, a full moon rose out of the ocean. Sometime during the early evening, the three newlywed couples did not return to the dance.

EPILOGUE

Elisabeth and John Howland – real people in real life - had 10 children together, all of whom lived to adulthood. They named their first daughter Desire, after Elisabeth's close friend who returned from Plymouth to England (or possibly Leiden, Holland) to find her mother. No records of Desire have been found in England or in Leiden, Holland.

Mary and John Winslow – real people in real life - had 10 children together, nine of whom lived to adulthood. They named their first daughter Susanna, possibly after John's sister-in-law and Mary's good friend, Susanna (White) Winslow.

The author would like to imagine that fictional characters, Hurit and Ahanu, kept in touch with Elisabeth and John. They visited in one another's homes, and the children from each family formed strong friendships. During the period of King Phillip's War in New England, 1675-76, Elisabeth's and John's son, Jabez, provided a haven for Hurit's and Ahanu's family in their home in Plymouth. Jabez's home really exists in modern-day Plymouth and is well worth a visit.

Rembrandt van Rijn is a real historical character. However, based on his fictional relationship with Elisabeth Tilley, the author would like to imagine that Rembrandt kept in touch with the Leiden Separatists to learn what he could about the fate of Elisabeth and those with whom she left Leiden. There has been speculation that in 1645, Rembrandt shipped several of his paintings overseas, but they were lost at sea. In the author's imagination, Rembrandt was sending the paintings to his first love, Elisabeth, in Plymouth.

Sources

3 October-Vereeniging. (2019). *International.* Retrieved from https://3october.nl/international

Architect of the Capitol. (2018). *Embarkation of the Pilgrims.* Retrieved from https://www.aoc.gov/art/historic-rotunda-paintings/embarkation-pilgrims

Bangs, J. (2014). *Pilgrim life in Leiden.* Leiden American Pilgrim Museum. Retrieved from http://www.leidenamericanpilgrimmuseum.org/Page31X.htm

Bethell, T. (1999). *How private property saved the pilgrims.* Hoover Digest. Retrieved from https://www.hoover.org/research/how-private-property-saved-pilgrims

Boroughs, J. J. (1997). *A new insight into the early settlement of Plymouth Plantation.* Retrieved from http://www.histarch.illinois.edu/plymouth/jbthesis.html

Ceremonial pipe. (2019). Retrieved from https://en.wikipedia.org/wiki/Ceremonial_pipe

COWASS North America. (2019). *Marriage or wedding ceremony.* Retrieved from http://www.cowasuck.org/lifestyle.cfm

Brooks, Rebecca B. (2011). *History of the Mayflower ship.* History of Massachusetts. Retrieved from https://historyofmassachusetts.org/the-mayflower/

Deetz, P. & Fennell, C. (2019). *Bradford's sketch of Plymouth.* The Plymouth Colony Archive Project. Retrieved from www.histarch.illinois.edu/plymouth/1620map.html

Didier, S. (2017). *How did the Indians tan deer hides?* Retrieved from https://www.theclassroom.com/how-did-the-indians-tan-deer-hides-12084320.html

Discover Gravesend (2019). Retrieved from http://www.discovergravesham.co.uk/gravesend-chronology/1610-1659.html

Earth Observatory. (2016). *Holland: First stop for the Pilgrims.* EOS Project Science Office. Retrieved from https://earthobservatory.nasa.gov/images/91317/holland-first-stop-for-the-pilgrims

Emmer, P. C. (2003). Review of *The Rise of Commercial Empires England and the Netherlands in the Age of Mercantilism, 1650-1770.* Retrieved from https://reviews.history.ac.uk/review/345

Encyclopedia of World Biography. (2019). *Samoset biography.* Retrieved from https://www.notablebiographies.com/supp/Supplement-Mi-So/Samoset.html

Encyclopedia of U.S. History. (2019). Plymouth Colony. Retrieved from https://www.encyclopedia.com/history/encyclopedias-almanacs-transcripts-and-maps/plymouth-colony

Foster, J. & Eccles, W. (2019). Fur trade. In *The Canadian Encyclopedia.* Retrieved from https://www.thecanadianencyclopedia.ca/en/article/fur-trade

Freedberg, W. (2018, July 23). *The ten craziest Massachusetts bird noises.* Retrieved from https://blogs.massaudubon.org/distractiondisplays/the-ten-craziest-massachusetts-bird-noises/

Gardening Know How. (2018). *Hazelnut picking: How and when to harvest hazelnuts.* Retrieved from https://www.gardeningknowhow.com/edible/nut-trees/hazelnut/when-to-harvest-hazelnuts.htm

History.com. (2009). *The pilgrims.* Retrieved from https://www.history.com/topics/colonial-america/pilgrims

Home Brew It. (2017). *How long does it take to brew your own beer?* Retrieved from https://www.homebrewit.com/blog/2010/07/01/how-long-does-it-take-to-brew-your-own-beer/

How colonists acquired title to land in Virginia. (2018). Retrieved from http://www.virginiaplaces.org/settleland/headright.html

Jamestown-Yorkton Foundation. (2006). *Jamestown settlement ships.* Retrieved from https://www.historyisfun.org/pdf/Jamestown-Ships/Jamestown_Ships_2013.pdf

Johnson, C. (2017). *MayflowerHistory.* Retrieved from http://mayflowerhistory.com

Jordans, Buckinghamshire. (2019). *The Mayflower barn.* Retrieved from https://en.wikipedia.org/wiki/Jordans,_Buckinghamshire

Kemp, T. J. (2018). Mayflower families across 12 generations: Finding the stories of your family in newspapers. Retrieved from https://www.genealogybank.com/static/downloads/Mayflower_Families_eBook.pdf

MedlinePlus. (2019). *Heat emergencies.* US National Library of Medicine. Retrieved from https://medlineplus.gov/ency/article/000056.htm

Ne-Do-Ba. (2014). *Exploring and sharing the Wabanaki history of interior New England.* Retrieved from http://www.nedoba.org/res_history.html

Older, C. L. (2010). *Documentation for Elizabeth Tilley.* Retrieved from http://www.cloldergen.com/public/page101/page101.html

Paul, H. (2014). *The myths that made America: An introduction to American Studies.* Bielefeld: Transcript Verlag. Retrieved from http://www.jstor.org/stable/j.ctv1wxsdq

Philbrick, N. (2006). *Mayflower: A story of courage, community, and war.* New York: Penguin Group.

Pilgrim Hall Museum. (2019). *Map of Plymouth Harbor by Samuel de Champlain, 1605.* Retrieved from https://www.pilgrimhall.org/pdf/Champlain_Map_and_Description.pdf

PlayShakespeare.com. (2016). *Globe Theater Information.* Retrieved from http://www.playshakespeare.com/license

Poetry Archive. (2019). *Landing of the Pilgrim Fathers.* Retrieved from https://www.poetry-archive.com/h/landing_of_the_pilgrim_fathers.html

Popular baby names, origin Native-American. (2019). Retrieved from https://adoption.com/baby-names/origin/Native-American

Raga, S. (2017, July 15). *15 facts about Rembrandt for his birthday.* Retrieved from http://mentalfloss.com/article/81770/15-facts-about-rembrandt-his-birthday

Russell, H.S. (1980). *Indian New England before the Mayflower.* Lebanon, NH: University Press of New England.

Samoset Biography. (2019). *Encyclopedia of World Biography*. Retrieved from http://www.notablebiographies.com/supp/Supplement-Mi-So/Samoset.html. Advameg, Inc.

Severy, M. (Ed.). (1962). *Men, ships, and the sea*. Washington, DC: National Geographic Society.

Shears, T. (no date). Photo of Welsh Springer Spaniel. License for use at https://creativecommons.org/licenses/by-sa/4.0/legalcode

Siteseen Limited. (2018). *Algonquian names*. Retrieved from https://www.warpaths2peacepipes.com/native-american-indian-names/algonquian-names.htm

Speedwell passenger list, 1620. (2004). http://sites.rootsweb.com/~mosmd/speedwell.htm

The girl in at by Rembradt.PNG. (2018, July 26). *Wikimedia Commons, the free media repository*. Retrieved from https://commons.wikimedia.org/w/index.php?title=File:The_Girl_in_a_Picture_Frame_by_Rembradt.PNG&oldid=312445106.

Van de Wetering, E. (2019). *Rembrandt van Rijn*. London: Encyclopedia Britannica. Retrieved from https://www.britannica.com/contributor/Ernst-van-de-Wetering/6225

Wikipedia. (2019). *Squanto*. Retrieved from https://en.wikipedia.org/wiki/Squanto#Captain_Weymouth%27s_voyage_and_the_first_kidnappings

Wolfinger, L.Q (producer), Collins, R. (writer), & Lindahl, C.H. (executive producer). (2006). *Desperate crossing: The untold story of the Mayflower* (Video). New York: The History Channel.

Yale Law School. (2008). The Third Charter of Virginia; March 12, 1611. The Avalon Project, Lillian Goldman Law Library. Retrieved from https://avalon.law.yale.edu/17th_century/va03.asp

About the Author

Ron Germaine was born in Lagos, Nigeria, and grew up in various towns throughout Ontario and Alberta, Canada. He was a high school teacher and counselor in British Columbia, Canada, and is currently Professor Emeritus, National University, La Jolla, California, where he worked with practicing teachers in a Master's program. He has published several professional journal articles and a book, *A concise guide to writing a thesis or dissertation: Educational research and beyond.*

Improbable Connections: A Mayflower Story is his first novel. Ron was drawn to learning more about the Mayflower because his mother passed down oral history that 'relatives came over on the Mayflower.' While a direct, ancestral link has not been established to those who came on the ship, 'cousin' relationships have been found with Elisabeth (Tilley) and John Howland, and with Mary (Chilton) and John Winslow.

Ron now lives in Abbotsford, British Columbia, near his five beautiful grandchildren and their remarkable parents: Matthew and Jessica, and Peter and Amanda.

Author's Contact Information

Dr. Ron W Germaine
rongermaine@hotmail.com

US Postal Address
Box 1690
534 Railway Avenue
Sumas, WA 98295

Canadian Postal Address
34785 Skyline Drive
Abbotsford, BC
V2S 1J2

CPSIA information can be obtained
at www.ICGtesting.com
Printed in the USA
LVHW112040291020
670186LV00004B/866